ARK OF BAPHOMET

James True

In memory of Tracy Twyman

CONTENTS

CHAPTER ONE

Valley of the Ka

In Homer's Iliad, Karnak was called "Thebes of the Hundred Gates." The famous valley of graveyards nearby wasn't the valley of the kings. It was called the Valley of the Gates of Kings. The word "gates" slumped out of the name over the years. I understand how the "Valley of the Kings" flows from the tongue, but the Valley of the Gates of Kings is where Kings enter and exit. You don't dwell on the threshold of your door. You certainly aren't buried there. Before the worshipping of kings, this place was the valley of the gates. The place where a mother would bury her baby's cord and placenta. No rational dynasty would bury sixty-two gold-plated mummies kilometers away from the world's most prestigious temple on its busiest river and call it discrete. The purpose of the Valley of the Gates of Kings was more practical than a graveyard. It was a wireless base station for one's ka while living.

This royal valley flows naturally off the clavicles of Mount Horn spilling into the western bank of the Nile. The ancient city of Karnak rests on its eastern bank, basking in its ions. Wādī Abwāb al-Mulūk translates as the "watercourse gate of the king," and we can't say much about its origin. The valley's

63 tombs date to 1600BC - 1100BC, but only a handful are accessible. The Nile has barely moved in 5,000 years. Egypt's continental plate rests independently on the waters of Sheol. Karnak has long been Egypt's root and Alexandria Egypt's flower.

The lotus survives thanks to its fleshy organ anchored in the river bed. The flower is tethered by a feeding tube from its muddy placenta stretching to the surface. The Nile suspends the lotus between two worlds. Ka is its root. Ba is its flower. Its life is the connection between as the water of life plucks its string like a harp. Like the flower, ba is dynamic. It is the living heart and the seat of your personality. Ba's flower opens every day. Ka is your root; it thrives in a foundation. Ba is wings; they thrive on mobility. When the Ka and Ba meet, you have Kabbalah.

When you eat the lotus, you place its magic in your belly. The effects make you forget your name. The name, or ren, is the intersection of ka and ba. On a cartouche, the name is encircled by a rope with a knot binding the letters to its meaning. One's name is this tether connecting you and your meaning. The Bible explains how God points Adam's eyes at the earth's creatures to activate his calibration routine.

He brought them to the man to see what he would name each one. And whatever the man called each living creature, that was its name. - Genesis 2:20

Ren is revealed in one's shadow. The shadow has the profound ability to shield the sun. It shows man his ka is formidable in the eyes of Ra. These are aspects of man: ka, ren, ba, and shadow (sheut). The ka, and thereby all parts of the soul, were installed and leveraged through these gates at Karnak. These sunken vaults were communal deposit boxes. Their long, slender hallways acted like antennae resonating through the horn of the mountain. There was nothing secret about these chambers. They were sacred.

The Valley of the Kings should be renamed the Valley of the Ka. It was a place where the soul was planted. Here, it was a magical crime to disturb the ka. Over time, these soul gardens were expanded deeper underground and eventually became exclusive mausoleums when the Pharaohs came in and took over the valley. Ka is not exclusive to kings. Ka is present in everyone and verified by Ra's shadow. Man is a living lotus. The Nile, Karnak, and the Valley of the Gates are ancient reminders there is more below the surface.

A child's dollhouse gives ka to its dolls. When a doll has a foundation, it makes it more pretend-able. Even in the backyard, the doll will have a footing in the world. Without a home, the doll withers from exposure. One does not truly travel without a home as context. The meaning of travel requires an origin point to build its definition. The expression, "you're a long way home" becomes meaningless without an origin. Click your heels and repeat after me, "There's no place like ka."

Phantom leg syndrome is ka. The root is still there, sending nutrients up the missing stalk. These nutrients form a ghost limb we still experience. The nerve pain from phantom limb syndrome is tangible. Mirror box therapy allows patients suffering from phantom limb syndrome to reunite with their ka. By placing their amputated limb behind a mirror, the patient can interact with the ka of their body and find relief.

Artificial reality is already in use as a therapeutic for trauma. Car accident victims can revisit the incident within a virtual space to allow the body to decrypt residual trauma. Shamans have employed these techniques for thousands of years. Ushabti dolls inside the underground chambers at the Gates of Kings do the same thing. The Egyptian opening of the mouth ceremony gave a totem life. The eyes, ears, nose, and mouth are routed to the ka. In folk magic, a poppet is stuffed inside the chimney and represents its owner. These totems were placeholders for ka. A popular version still in use today is the teddy bear. We've reduced ka to the imagination, but energy is vital to the immune system. We would be sleepwalking in a society that rejected its practice.

They say emotions carry in the hips, and yoga is known to release them. There are four petals around the perimeter of the lotus that opens its flower each day. In man, this is the poly vagus. The vagus nerve is the tenth cranial nerve, binding every organ to a single river. Egypt is the body, and the vagus has two branches connecting its upper and lower kingdoms. The dorsal branch is the root of the lotus connecting the liver, stomach, and intestines. The ventral branch is the flower controlling its face, heart, and lungs. These nerves intersect at the body's cartouche, the voice box.

The original name for Thebes was Waset or scepter. A scepter is a royal cane. Like the umbilical cord, it connects the king to the land. Luxor Temple was not dedicated to a god or king. It was a center for a king's rejuvenation and was known as the southern sanctuary. Luxor greets the valley of gates like a doula birthing in the Nile. During Opet, Luxor receives the sacred barge with the venerated statues of Adam and Eve. Once called Amun and Mut, they made the first carnal child, or scepter, and named him Khonsu, otherwise known as Cain. Thebes is his namesake. He commits the first murder, his brother Osiris. Adam was even older than Thebes. Before Thebes had Amun, Heliopolis had Atum. Heliopolis was the land of the obelisk. An entire city dedicated to the magic of the phallus. Amun and Atum are the self-creating Adam. The Adam before Adam and Eve.

The sarcophagus is preservation. It was an ark of resurrection. The longer a body remained undisturbed, the longer its ka persisted. This is the technology of tombstones.

Dead men live on in the soil of beating hearts. To know someone's name is to give their ka a place to flower. In Egypt, death was a birth. Sarcophagus was a later term from the Greeks, meaning flesh swallower. The Egyptians referred to the coffin as the egg.

The body is emptied, and its organs are placed into jars. The heart remains in its chest with a single scarab beetle. The hollow, naked vessel is coated with salt, which sits for a moon to absorb and infuse all its memories. The body is swaddled in linens from the family and placed inside its egg, or neb ankh. This vessel, this ark named ankh, was a life possessor, not a coffin.

The Amduat is a recovered funeral text that outlines the twelve gates, or hours, through the underworld. The Valley of the Gates of Kings was essential to this journey. These are the footsteps into the underworld. If you imagine its first step in Karnak, you can trace this journey from the eastern banks of the Nile up into the valley and back across. You can still see the sandy island of Seker today on the western part of the Nile at Karnak. This is referenced in hour four of the journey and again in hour nine. All of this culminated back at Karnak for hour eleven when the eyes were opened.

The Gates of Amduat
> *Hour 1 - Enter western horizon from day into night.*
> *Hour 2-3 - Pass through the waters of Osiris.*
> *Hour 4 - Sandy realm of Seker, hawk, maze, snake-boat.*
> *Hour 5 - Enters Mount Horn, Tomb of Osiris, lake of fire.*
> *Hour 6 - High noon. Serpent wraps body. Resurrection.*
> *Hour 7 - The snake is subdued with chains.*
> *Hour 8 - Tomb is open (He is risen).*
> *Hour 9 - Leaves Seker by rowing back into the water.*
> *Hour 10 - More water.*
> *Hour 11 - Eyes restored at Karnak.*

Hour 12 - Back on Eastern horizon.

There are ten gates or pylons at the temples of Eve and Adam in Karnak. The Amduat ritual was condensed inside the grounds of the temple. There's even a sacred lake inside the central precinct of Amen-Ra. So much has happened to the ceremony over the millennium, but you can still see its roots as an ancient birthing site.

The Old Testament's Tabernacle in the Wilderness was a portable model of Luxor Temple. The original Holy of Holies was the Chapel of the Wind. A shrine of Alexander the Great would eventually conquer this space. The followers of YHW of the Shasu, a wandering slave tribe, used it as inspiration for their Holy of Holies. These nomadic slaves made their exodus from Egypt and pilfered its ceremonies. Astrology was taught at Luxor and a few miles north at Dendera. Every constellation of the zodiac is there on its ceilings. So are the stories of Adam and Eve and the tribulations of Cain and Able. Akhenaten tried to pilfer Egypt's past too. But you can never erase Egypt. The ka from its pen is too black to wash.

The opposite of tomb raiding is tomb enriching. No one talks about this, but it happens. It used to be the norm. Consider the pagan mounds as one of many examples. Shrines have always been communal. Tomb enriching is the idea one would find a tomb of coveted treasure and add something to it instead of taking it away. Why is this such a challenging idea to fathom? Even today, burial mounds are communal. The community is what gives them power. This is why kings wanted to be buried in the valley.

Think about how hard it would be to dig a tomb for months secretly. The Valley of the Gates of Kings was a communal mound under the protection of the mountain's pyramid-shaped horn next to the Nile. This was a holy place activated when someone was born and the valley where everyone's spirit could be safely revered and stored.

There is a ceremony called the Stretching of the Cord used by the pharaohs to commence a new building. Doulas practiced this same ritual in the birthing ceremony. The invention of baptism came from this ritual in the Nile. The cord was kept in the Valley of the Gates as a living vessel for their newborn king. Before hieroglyphics, the birth cord was the cartouche. It was stretched and tied into a knot in a ceremony and guarded by reverence, not secrecy. In the beginning, the valley of the gates had no gold, only priceless treasure.

CHAPTER TWO

The Vitruvian Adam

In 1490, Leonardo da Vinci created a drawing of primordial Adam. The figure bearing double arms and legs exposes Adam's chimeric nature. Notice the feet. One pair stands on the base of a square, while the other is on a circle's circumference. This is a brilliant way of representing two manifestations sharing a single form. The sketch was Leonardo's reflection on the works of the Roman architect Vitruvius. The passages Leonardo quotes boom like a decree from a podium, "The ideal body is eight heads high. A palm is four fingers. A man is twenty-four palms." Leonardo did more than contemplate these ratios. He added a singularly perfect illustration of the chimeric man as the epicenter of golden proportions.

A chimera is a single organism composed of cells with more than one distinct genotype or zygote. Simplified, this is two unique DNA living in a single body. Plants, animals, and humans all have this capacity for dual occupancy. The human body can house two unique DNA, two immune systems, and even two bloodstreams. This fact is not a mutation. It's a feature that's been with us from the beginning. The body can host four unique genotypes in the hermaphrodite or tetragametic chimera. Chimera work like nesting dolls but with twins. Chimeras are not genetic anomalies. They show us an ancient footprint from our genetic past. They reveal the blueprint of our capacity as a genetic instrument. They shed light on how we got here and possibly even why.

Before Adam and Eve, there was Ædam, the protoplast or the first-formed. He is the primal hermaphrodite and the sacred androgyne. This is the complete man, including the parts that aren't visible. We call this the Vitruvian Adam. Jung might call this the integrated psyche. Man is the Vitruvian Adam who has been cleaved or split. Man's fall from Eden is a genetic process unwinding itself through time. It is the process of birth above and below. This split invented duality. It opened the floodgates and took us to a new world where our consciousness cracked open the doors.

Carl Jung would call the Vitruvian Adam the integrated psyche. Man's occulted or missing sex organs were his anima. The woman's occulted half is her animus. The anima and animus make their way into mythology. Lilith was Adam's ghost. Even discussing these ideas is difficult in a culture where we ignore and parody intangible concepts. We need to resurrect terms from the past to use them as utensils. Classical Mandaic literature called this ghost Adam Kasia, or the hidden Adam. Likewise, Hawa Kasia was the invisible Eve. Adam Pagria would be the bodily Adam, the one you see. Note how Adam is given a spirit and a soul:

The creator and Ptahil created Adam Pagria with his helpers, the Seven Planets and the Twelve Zodiacs, from clay and other elements. With the help of Ruha, Ptahil gave Adam Pagria the spirit. Manda d-Hayyi and Hibil Ziwa gave the lightworld soul (Adam Kasia) to the body. Hawa was then created as a companion for the first bodily Adam.

* * *

The Vitruvian Adam lacked dimension because he was so complete. This paradox is the driving force of growth and reproduction. We have recently gained new capacities that will help us remember Vitruvian Adam. The technology of CRISPR and GMOs have given us context to conceive how something like this would be likely or even possible. As we track the footprints of a creator, we slowly discover they resemble our own. This leads us to conclude that neither the chicken nor the egg was created; they were spawned.

CHAPTER THREE

The Hills have Giants

For some time, society has shunned the idea of a giant version of man. We say it's impossible despite acknowledging it in other species. Birds, bats, mice, cats, lizards, fish, insects, and plants can be giants, but not man. That's a sacred line we do not cross. These kinds of taboos are always the best clues to uncovering painful history. You learn to use them as a dowsing rod to mine new wisdom. The rarest treasurers will always be found where no one is looking, which is why taboo is such a marvelous compass.

The hills have giants. This word traverses every continent and language despite how much our history tries to forget. Columbus did not discover America; he erased it. But the giants are still here, and their shoulders prop up our heels. We buried Atlas in a box and labeled him a lizard, but the giants remain. They say Osama Bin Laden was as tall as two towers. His body was so heavy it fell into the sea from a helicopter. The splash was a giant mission accomplished.

The pen is a sword with etiquette. We are flawless in our assassination of history and will civilize every artery using its blade. Both the Sun Dance and Ghost Dance are forbidden by etiquette. Every potlatch turns into florescent dust under etiquette's blade. Every valley went unnamed and reclaimed by etiquette. But the mounds were always here and will always remain haunted by giants.

His name was Bearfoot. He wore a broad cape of draped skins covering his frame from neck to toe. Their brown and black pelts glistened like an ice forest from the cold river's mist. He was as tall as the trees and could pluck Smith's head from its shoulders like an apple. Even sitting on a stump, he was as tall as the Captain stood. The Indian assured the interpreter he understood their question. His tongue rolled out its answer like molasses from his deep bass, "No river runs west to any ocean."

Captain Smith paid diligence to the meaning and urged his translator, "Ask him how he knows so we can see if he's dumb." The interpreter drew a circle in the dirt around the sketch of the turtle and poked footsteps connecting Captain Smith's feet to the map. Grasping a pinch of earth, the interpreter pulls it to his lips, speaking the word for food in six dialects. Bearfoot nodded that he understood. He pointed his staff to the turtle's left arm, saying, "People of the clear salt water." Bearfoot then drew a terrain of ridges down the turtle's back and began to teach the Captain how the Great Divide traversed the Rockies and separated the waters from the waters. Still, he wasn't sure if Captain Smith had the intelligence to understand him.

In 1677, Robert Plot wrote,

"There happily came to Oxford while I was writing of this, a living Elephant to be shown publickly with whose Bones I compared ours and found those of the Elephant not only of a different Shape but also incomparably different to ours. It remains they must have been the bones of Men or Women."

His entry came before the idea of terrible lizards, or what we know today as dinosaurs. Robert was a meticulous collector, and this well-trained Oxford professor declared he had proof of giants. Today, we insist it was the distal end of a femur from Megalosaurus. We insist Robert was mistaken. But the specimen mentioned in his notes has been swallowed by time. A million-dollar market would bloom from America's graveyard in the next two centuries. Thousands of burial mounds left fallow by the indigenous would be unearthed and auctioned as more "terrible lizards."

Before snake oil, there was lizard oil. The selling of mislabeled relics is an ancient profession, and the tallest tale wins. Ask Sauroposeidon. Even today, a Dutch museum insists a rock allegedly brought home from the Moon turned out to be a piece of petrified wood. NASA confirms hundreds of these objects were handed to foreign countries as gifts. The question is not whether dinosaur bones are real. The question is whether they prove giants impossible, which they do not—quite the contrary.

Every region of early American history has giants planted in its mythology. Mythology doesn't make these stories untrue. It simply means the idea of giants was known by several cultures that had no contact with each other. Most of these giants are described as cannibals or humanoid beasts, and they tended to feast on children and grew fanatic near menstruating women. There is a symbiosis with these giants, as if it was quite natural to live among creatures who could eat your children if you weren't vigilant.

The number and diversity of these stories go far beyond the reach of simple storytelling for children's sake. The cross-culture outline is consistent — people form a community and take action against barbaric giants. Most burial mounds in the eastern states were considered untouchable by local tribes because they believed them to contain the bones of a different race. Documented as far north as the Arctic circle all the way south into Argentina, describe these giants as progenitors here to sow, or copulate, the seed of future man before disappearing into the ground.

The Aztec giants were called the Quinametzin. They lived during the first sun, a half sun. They fed off acorns and lacked pride. Jaguars eventually devoured them at the close of the first sun. Mixcoatl, the Aztec version of the Greek deity Uranus, bore six sons, all of whom were giants. They were here to populate the earth after the great flood. The Noah's Ark of Mesoamerica included a giant starter race, a great deluge, and a chosen family preserved to repopulate. The gods punished these Aztec Nephilim because they did not venerate them properly. Their civilization ended as a result of great calamities and as a punishment from the heavens for the sins they committed. The same giant story is seeded in the soil of every continent.

The Tarahumara lived with giants in the highlands of northern Mexico. In 1890, Carl Lumholtz led his first expedition into their territory. In his book Unknown Mexico, Carl quotes one of the locals describing the giants, "They were as big as pine trees with heads as big as boulders. They taught the Tarahumaras how to plant corn by cutting down trees and burning them, but they ate children." He recorded their testimony.

"From Wasivori came giants to Nararachic to ask alms. Tesvino [a beer made from corn] they liked very much. They worked very fast, and the Tarahumaras put them to hoe and weed the corn, and gave them food and tesvino. But the giants were fierce, and ravished the women while the latter were under the influence of the Moon; therefore the Tarahumaras got very angry and they mixed a decoction made from the chilicote-tree with the corn that they gave the giants to eat, and the giants died."

* * *

The giants of Aad from present-day Saudi Arabia were famous for their physical strength. They carved their houses into the side of mountains and took out trees with their hands. They faced the same fate as the Nephilim.

As for Aad, they were arrogant upon the earth without right and said, "Who is greater than us in strength?" Did they not consider that Allah who created them was greater than them in strength? But they were rejecting Our signs. - Quran 41:15

Old Testament scholars acknowledge their flood stories contradict each other when viewed from a lens of a singular event. Aztec cosmology has five suns and five creations, not one. There is no contradiction. The Biblical story is a compression of the death of many worlds reduced to a single reset story for mass consumption. Even Egypt has three distinct dynasties, all reigning in splendor for thousands of years, only to be wholly toppled and reset unexplainably in a matter of a few hundred. These dynasties collapsed on top of themselves, deluge after deluge, before they could fully recover. These footprints show how the ark was a technology of necessity spurred by the devastating hammer of the gods that continued to strike humanity blow after blow.

The Codex Vaticanus depicts the Nahua flood story featuring a tower, giants, and an ark all on one parchment. Many argue this is Christian doctrine subverting itself into Mesoamerica, but when you look at the Olmec, Maya, and Aztec records, you see even more flesh in the story. The process of reinstalling man after a calamity requires many suns. History tells us this is a messy process, and we see its dirty trail all over mythology.

In pre-Inca Peru, Viracocha[1] rose from Lake Titicaca during the time of darkness and said, "Let there be light." He made the sun, the moon, and the stars. He created mankind by breathing into stones. He destroyed his first creation of brainless giants with a flood to make humans. Like always, humans were upgraded from the giants. He erased the people around Lake Titicaca with a great flood lasting sixty days, saving two humans to reboot civilization. Like Adam and Eve, they gave names to all the world's trees, flowers, fruits, and herbs. From Greece to Peru to Alaska, we see the same syncretic mythology.

The giants of the Old Testament had natal charts, death records, and detailed family trees. King Og of Bashan was the last survivor of the Rephaite giants. His bed measured thirteen feet long. Nephilim, Emim, Rephaim, Giborim, Zamzumim, Anakim, and Avim were all giant clans or families. Goliath was a Rephaim brought up in Gath. The city was an ancient stronghold of the Anakim, suggesting Goliath may have had Anakim relatives. His recorded height was from seven to eleven feet tall. The National Library of Medicine hosts a study describing Goliath as a candidate for pituitary tumors typical of hereditary gigantism[2]. The word " Rephaim" means "the dead" in most modern biblical translations. But the original meaning is "buried in the depths of Sheol." Sheol is the Bible's word for the collective unconscious, our forgotten past. All past is memory. Everything known and forgotten is stored in the salt of Sheol's waters. This passage from Isaiah is translated in the King James Version as a reference to "Hell," but the Hebrew

---

[1] The word "Viracocha" translates as "sea foam" harkening to the same relationship between Mixcoatl and Uranus who birthed Aphrodite from his castrated scrotum's sea foam.

[2] PMC4113151

word Sheol would be better understood in this verse as "Your ancestors."

Hell beneath hath been troubled at thee, To meet thy coming in, It is waking up for thee Rephaim, All chiefs ones of earth, It hath raised up from their thrones All kings of nations. - Isaiah 14:9

It's no surprise King James decided to call his ancestors "Hell." This was a king who wrote a manual on the etiquette of burning witches. Once man ran out of giants, he turned his torch to the witch. The Devil was born from a quest to blame something for the deluge. The hunting of giants fueled Rome's political campaigns. The rise of Alexander was built on the defeat of giants like King Porus, the seven-foot-tall elephant rider, and the barbarian celts of the Adriatic Sea.

Giganticide is a lucrative business inside and outside of scripture. Our past was a world dominated by the fear of a berserker. A wilderness full of feral human changelings immersed in a predator trance is a dilating reality. This past is too terrifying to remember so we blot it out. Melanin is chemical amnesia administered in the body to remain buoyant in an experience. We will only remember what etiquette allows. This filter has added up over the centuries.

When we see giants today, we label them psychopathic. We tell ourselves it's a deviation from the human design. It's easy to see why we would sweep this under the rug. It's an essential part of our survival mechanism to sever the cord from our primitive ooze. If we had not despised the past, we'd still live in its slop. This passage from Proverbs is printed with the literal translation showing the deep psychological distaste we hold for our roots.

The woman named Folly is loud; she is naive and knows nothing. She sits at the door of her house, on a seat in the heights of the city, calling out to those who pass by, who make their paths straight. "Whoever is simple, let him turn in here!" she says to him who lacks judgment. "Stolen water is sweet, and bread eaten in secret is tasty!" But they do not know that the Rephaim are there, that her guests are in the depths of Sheol. - Proverbs 9:13-18

We have castrated our ka. We didn't exterminate the giants; we buried them alive. A giant was rooted in his lower kingdom—the land of the red king. The home of Muladhara is the four-petaled lotus controlling the opening and closing of the crown. These are the pillars of the earth, and it's hard to look down from where we are now. Who we were then lacked the calories to support something as extravagant as the ego. Today's human thinks of himself as an "I," but the giant thought of himself as "me." His neocortex was rudimentary, which explained his brutish behavior.

They will all respond to you, saying, "You too have become weak, as we are; you have become like us!" Your pomp has been brought down to Sheol, along with the music of your harps. Maggots are your bed and worms your blanket. - Isaiah 14:11

The Greek word for ego translates to mean "I am." To hate the ego is to hate the man who rose above his pelvis. The war on giants is a war on our past. The word "herem" is a type of dedicatory vow that is irrevocable and unredeemable. This is a mortal censor requiring complete obliteration. The Catholics share a similar idea in the term vitandus. Information is excommunicated from a community under the auspices of the greater good. This doesn't have to be a conscious pursuit for it to be something we practice every day.

Then Israel made this vow to the Lord: "If you will deliver these people into our hands, we will totally destroy their cities." - *Numbers 21:2*

The irrevocable giving over of something to the Lord requires complete annihilation, typically by fire. We don't have a concept like this in our vocabulary, which makes it hard to recognize it even exists. We could never imagine blatantly erasing something from our history despite the fact we did it with giants.

"Yet I destroyed the Amorites before them, though they were tall as the cedars and strong as the oaks. I destroyed their fruit above and their roots below." - Amos 2:9

Giants don't have to be tall. In Greek and Roman mythology, the Gigantes were known as a race of great strength and aggression, not size. They constantly struggled with the Olympian gods and were a constant source of disappointment. Apparently, the gods were expecting perfection from their giants and didn't get it. But this thinking is contradicted by its mythology because a family is preserved and deemed worthy of replanting in every giant story. The heirloom human suggests the phase of carnal giants worked exactly as expected, and the time of the giants was a known step in the process.

It's easy to see man cling to the idea God would never kill something he loved. But this happens in every greenhouse and on every farm every day. These stories are more than mythology. They are the missing link between how we got here and what we are willing to admit. Hominid evolution is proven by the Old Testament, not denied. Every ancient scripture about the giants is a secondary reference. But man employs the jujitsu of science and denialism to ease the pain from the jungle. The closest he can get to giants is by dressing them in the costume of Neanderthal and Cro-Magnon. It is the reset of civilization that science still struggles to accept.

In 1873, Heinrich Schliemann found the "mythological" city of Troy, and now it's a part of reality. Acceptance collapses the wave of mythology and opens its floodgates to a world of trauma we were actively working to forget. Mythology is the opium that allows the truth to be in the room while remaining oblivious to its acceptance. If you place a bird on an island with no predator, the bird grows large. The same thing happens with fish in a pond. As it turns out, gigantism occurs in every species, including mammals and primates. Man is sizable to his terrain; this feature is the norm, not the exception.

On May 4, 1908, the New York Times published a story that the skeletal remains of 200 giants were found in Mexico. The article is still on file with the publication and was never retracted. By 1908, dinosaurs were booming, and every bone was sucked into its wake. Like any science, archeology has its rudder in fashion. Ideas with charisma are always the first to be validated. This turns out to be a palatable form of censorship that occurs quite naturally.

In many cases, a debate becomes too tiresome for a muscle to endure, and the collective psyche will pick a winner and move on. The collective consciousness is a growing plasma with a finite attention span and capacity. Our desktop isn't big enough for giants.

In 1845, Albert Koch unveiled his dinosaur, Hydrarchos, which turned out to be a mashup of several whale skeletons. On December 18, 1912, Charles Dawson convinced the Geological Society of London and the British Museum that his Piltdown Man was the missing link. Science embraced Dawson's jawbone as the proof man came from a monkey, and for fifty long years, no one corrected it. The Scopes Monkey Trial of 1925 proved it didn't even matter.

Lying is a vital part of the immune system. It regulates the flow of vagus energy to the upper and lower kingdoms. The activated parts of the brain when we lie are the same ones activated when we heal. Lying is spell craft. It generates a transformative field that warps reality. Lying ceases to be immoral under consent. Under consent, lies become medicine that nurtures one's field. The spell "Everything is going to be okay" is a lie medicine. Even using our imagination is an art of lying.

The most common congenital hand normality today is polydactylism (polydactyly). This is when a baby is born with one or more extra fingers. Statistics for cases today are one in 500 but seem to appear more frequently in the past. Polydactyly and gigantism are documented in ancient scripture.

In still another battle, which took place at Gath, there was a huge man with six fingers on each hand and six toes on each foot — twenty-four in all. He also was descended from Rapha. - 1 Chronicles 20:6

In Chaco Canyon, New Mexico, one of the largest Ancestral Puebloan Bonito sites birthed 96 skeletons, and 3% of them demonstrated polydactyly. That's fifteen times the number of cases from today's statistics. Extra toes found on the skeletons were adorned with turquoise. Canyon murals feature six-digit handprints and footprints. Hundreds of miles away in Arizona, a polydactyly infant burial site features a clay-lined grave suggesting adoration of the infant. Additional locations in Texas and the four corners feature many more examples of the same prevalence and respect for what's supposed to be a rare anomaly.

Postaxial polydactyly is defined by the extra toe or finger

forming on the outside of the foot. This is the most common form of polydactyly compared to central or preaxial polydactyly, which are hundreds of times rarer. It seems as if what we have labeled a genetic deformity is more a remnant of a design we outgrew. Or, in this case, out-shrunk. The bias shows itself when we consider the coccyx is labeled an abandoned tail instead of a defective bone growth. Gigantism and polydactyly are more natural than we understand. The vast reduction in the number of polydactyly cases today compared to just 1500 years ago suggests something is unfolding in our genetic code. Perhaps this is why Down Syndrome is negatively associated with postaxial polydactyly. The data tells us having a sixth finger or toe does not express itself like normal mutations of the hands and toes. We are new to the science of genes and haven't recognized our own bias.

Maximinus Thrax was emperor of Rome for three years. His team described him as a semi-illiterate barbarian commander. Ancient Roman writers claimed he stood over eight feet tall. His thumb was so large that he wore his wife's bracelet as a ring.

"He was, in any case, a man of such frightening appearance and colossal size that there is no obvious comparison to be drawn with any of the best-trained Greek athletes or warrior elite of the barbarians." - Herodian

Scaphocephaly was made famous by Pharaoh Akhenaten. His boat-shaped head is a condition known as sagittal craniosynostosis. Like postaxial polydactyly, sagittal craniosynostosis is also considered a defect blamed on a premature fusion of skull sutures. But this condition also spreads the weight of the brain and skull forward and aft away from the neck, allowing more weight distribution.

This idea is complemented by the genetic anomaly known as the cervical rib. Like postaxial polydactyly, it is common in many people. One in every 200 people has this extra rib growing at the base of the neck just above the collarbone. This neck rib is considered a congenital overdevelopment in the spine despite always being found on the seventh cervical vertebra. In reptiles, the cervical rib is credited with making gigantism possible. Without it, they would lack the strength to raise their enormous head.

It is not uncommon for human genes to dramatically change their expression. Ask Elizabeth French, the horned woman. Cornu cutaneum is the ability of the skin to grow horns. She was born at Tenterden in Kent. Employed as a sitter, she had a horn at the back of her head ten inches long. Mr. Fauks hired her for many years until she broke her horn and sold it to Sir Hans Sloane. The genetic secrets from our past suffocate when we demonize them. As we learn more about these ancient capabilities, we unlock our potential and emerge as children of Prometheus.

One of the most misunderstood giants was the Cyclops. These weren't one-eyed men, literally. Being a craftsman requires depth perception, and monovision will create many accidents around the forge. The Cyclops were Nephilim who saw reality through the pineal or first eye. We all do this, but man has developed a skill where he lies to himself about it coming through his eyeballs. The amygdala is a trickster. It's part of its job, so we won't freeze in shock the next time Zeus walks by. Cyclops vision has no amygdala filter. The Cyclops were contractors for Zeus, and they had to be able to look him in the eye. Filtering the boss only hurts workflow and threatens productivity.

Cyclops performs poorly against every man he encounters. Cyclops spends most of his time making gifts for others. They made Zeus' thunderbolt, Poseidon's trident, and the cap of invisibility. They erected the megalithic walls for society from China to Peru despite having no interest in civilization. Culture is a world of subtle deceit and flattery, and Cyclops lacked the equipment to see these falsities. When Odysseus told the Cyclops his name was "nobody," the Cyclops believed him. Pineal vision makes a Cyclops gullible, not dumb. They were loners forging our infrastructure for free, and we repaid their generosity by thanking each of them with a free eye stick.

What the Cyclops saw threatened us. They drank raw source reality through their first eye, which terrifies man. They carry an unfiltered memory through the deluge. We must poke each of them with an eye sword to stop the leak. The Cyclops of Odysseus was Polyphemus. His name meant "abounding in songs and legends." Polyphemus was a link to the past, and he had to go.

While the Cyclops were vulnerable to manipulation and struggled with a nasty habit of cannibalism, this does not mean they lacked wisdom. The Cyclops was as gifted as they were strong and carried the time capsule of ancient wisdom in their genes. Their resources fed Odysseus and his men when they were shipwrecked. Cyclops were children of Poseiden, and man emerged safe from their world, protected in the belly of its sheep.

These giants knew their days were over, yet they forged us a new world anyway. The mythology reflects their willingness and duty to embrace this destiny. You see a changing of the guard from giants to man in the dynasties of Egypt. Its monumental architecture was collapsing while its culture and writing flourished. This trend is not limited to Egypt. The city of Teotihuacan showed the same trend.

The Cyclops story is worldwide. In Irish mythology, they were called Fomorians. Balor, the talented castle builder, had an eye so threatening it scorched the earth when he opened it.

Balor tried as best as he could to cover the eye using nine pieces of leather, but alas, he befell the same fate when a spear was thrust into his eye by a human.

CHAPTER FOUR

Hushing of Hashem

To name something is to own it. Hence man's never-ending quest to name God. He shouts this name in battle and uses its letters to kill. He invokes it in the passions of pleasure and pain. As man's squire, God's name must be resilient. It must be capable of carrying its champion across the deepest ocean and the coldest moat. The random word won't do. The name of God is a circuit, and the letters that pull the most amps will reign supreme.

Belemnite is an extinct order of squid-like cephalopods with a skeletal structure extending into its cone. Millions of years ago, it would hunt small prey with ten barbed tentacles. Belemnite's name from Ancient Greek means dart or arrow. As a fossil, its calcitic phallus was revered as one of the earliest known symbols of divinity. Tracing back to 3100 BC, its opalized remains were venerated as the Egyptian deity Min. Shamelessly nude, Min was rendered in solid black skin, grasping his fully erect penis with his left hand while brandishing a flail with his right. Min was a God that predated reverence. It was the divine urge manifested into a workable symbol for early man.

Symbols are words for the mind. Their language needs no

teacher. Their pictographic nature conveys the same photons of understanding we find in the world. An erect phallus held a meaning understood by every village. The vibration of its definition was felt as power. Every icon, symbol, or word is a battery charged with recognition. The recognition has a customized flavor we recall in the hippocampus. We were born to eat symbols like fruit. They are the template God uses to build himself a home in our mind.

Understanding consciousness as emergent requires us to see man in a kind of neurological childhood. The collective mind of any family, tribe, or civilization builds itself on the sharing of its meanings. Symbols raise consciousness out of the ground like seeds from the underworld. You can feel consciousness growing through its recognition of meanings in the garden. Meaning is a nutrient in the soil. Therefore witness is a sunlight that gives man's seed its desire to unfurl. Man's social nature gives him a never-quenching desire to recognize his meanings in each other. We are not real until our meanings are complete. This is a completely different reality from the Cyclops. We are rendering a creation that could not have existed in a simpler construct.

The mind expands into itself like a universe. Concepts like civilization, morality, and love are intangible, so it is hard to recognize how much they shape-shift as we grow. Comprehending the supernatural is a skill we acquired with lots of practice. Today's man is neither static nor complete. Nor was he twelve or even two hundred generations ago. He is an iteration of himself seasoned by his terrarium. He is in a state of constant upgrade. Every new generation expands the complexity of its soil for a new dimension of concepts. Having a name is an advanced concept in the mind of a raccoon. Having a God is an advanced concept in the early mind of man. His conceptual "me" evolves into "I" when he grows resilient enough to flower an ego. This is the move from giant, the me, to man, the I.

At his root, man is a phallus on feet. And so it is no different with his concept of God. But this fossilized phallic deity lacked the power of mobility. Want and need are a primal fuel produced inside everything alive. This is the fundamental meaning of the word erection, which is why its found at the root of every god. Once God rises, he is ready to walk.

The Anguiped is a Greco-Roman deity with legs in the form of serpents. The creature was featured on talismans found all across the eastern Mediterranean. One of the more popular versions of the anguiped was the Abraxas. Abraxas bears the head of a rooster, the torso of a man, and the legs of a serpent. He inherited the flail from Min and served man as a more suitable diety for the times. The anguiped is still alive today in mermaids and coffee shop logos. It fulfilled its purpose of moving the primordial God out of the depths of the ocean. God, as a creation, evolved. Man, as a creation, was spawned. People get these things reversed sometimes.

The success of the anguipeds reflects the era's appetite. The mash-up of serpent, man, and beast was fresh real estate on a budding consciousness. The old symbol of an obelisk or a phallus was too static and rudimentary. Anguipeds combined the flair and mobility of sea tentacles with the bold head of a rooster in the comfort of a human-skinned torso. These custom deities were cathedrals carried on the body because God wasn't ready for a church. He was an infant who needed to suckle against the skin of its mother.

The technology of a talisman is rooted in the owner's electricity drawing its power from his field and broadcasting it like a beacon. When a stranger recognizes his talisman, he sends energy into it, and the owner feels the benefit. The owner witnesses the power of his talisman in the face of a stranger, which powers the talisman even more. This exchange is an early expression of the circuit of God pulling amps into its capacitor. As man's consciousness unfolds, so does the range and resiliency of his God's plasma.

Abraxas was the first devil created from the shaming of Priapus. Teenage boys practice his prayer every morning on the school bus while cursing their erection back into the bowels of hell. The giant from the black lagoon must be subdued to preserve civilization. A century and a half before the teachings of Christ, Yahweh's name was portrayed below the image of a cock-headed man. It was spelled then as IAO, which would become IAOEU, and finally, YAHWEH. The time of Abraxas unleashed a free market on sigil magic. Letters and words became as powerful as the symbols which reigned before them. More importantly, the community sprouted like berries around their interpretation and encryption. Man's attachment to the community would grow complicated once he whetted his appetite for a universal God.

As a fledgling deity, Yahweh grew up in the wilderness. His followers were the nomads of YHW. Known by Amenhotep III and later by Ramses II as the Shasu of YHW, the nomadic slave tribe wandering the land seeking a master and wreaking havoc on anyone who agreed to take them. About thirty-five deities in the Old Testament were directly competing with Yahweh. Yahweh swallowed them all.

Yahweh is the incorporated legion of many spirits seated at a single table. This is the boardroom of the Elohim. Adam was made in Elohim's image. Elohim refers to himself as plural and calls himself "that." When you dissect the Elohim, you find a genderless, soupy plurality.

And God said unto Moses, I Am That I Am: and he said, Thus shalt thou say unto the children of Israel, I Am hath sent me unto you. - Exodus 3:14

* * *

The Hebrew translation of Elohim is "yoked to a singular spirit over the waters." Human life begins in the blastocyst after fertilization when a cavity surrounded by a ball of 16 cells is flooded with water. Those 16 cells forming that cavity are the Elohim. The Elohim are you. In the beginning it was you who created the heavens and the earth. You made all this and called it good.

To know God's name is to conceive his place. He is the plasma of everyone's beliefs uploaded to the cloud. Every war, every crusade, every scapegoat, and every sacrifice was made in his name and all of that energy is stored in his batteries. Every Bible in every hotel room waits in a drawer to collect energy into its offering plate. The power of Yahweh is the power of his consensus and plurality.

All of Yahweh's plasma is centralized into a chain of command. As God grew more complex, so did his root structure in unconsciousness. When the brain creates a personality, it builds agency. These agents compete with each other to carry signals of witness. As consciousness forms, agents conglomerate and collapse into an agreement, and that agreement is you. The Elohim works the same way.

Abram became Abraham. Sarai became Sarah. YHW became YHWH. The extension "ha" promoted each of them as an agent of authority. It raises them and frames them in the window of "ha," preserving them as icons in the collective hypothetical. This is the anatomy of the unconscious. Yahweh required a foundation to build his church inside, and Simon, the reed, petrified into Peter, the rock.

Something funny happens when you centralize a deity. Suddenly your campaign to tell the people everything you can about God turns into a quest to hide it. If the name of God was a living market, the Tabernacle in the Wilderness was a functioning barbecue in its food court. The smell of freshly cooked meat drew a crowd like any revival. Once inside, you discover there's an inner tent, and you want to know more.

The marketing genius of the tabernacle model is undeniable. It functioned on a belief engine centralized around the ritual of animal sacrifice. To believe in the ritual charged a secret golden box inside a secret holy tent inside another secret, even more, holy tent. The reverence and encryption deployed formed a three-tiered belief antenna for broadcasting. As God unfurled this antenna, he moved his ka out of the talisman and into the temple. His tabernacle requires his name to be known and hidden simultaneously.

The Mothers of Reading are four Semitic consonants used to indicate a vowel. These magic letters carry a dual-gendered power. In Hebrew, these letters are alef, he, waw, and yodh. The Hebrew name for God is composed of these letters. Each letter is male and female simultaneously. These letters contain the secret name of God. Its understanding is only decrypted through the attention one pays to its secret. One studies things to worship them. When we strive to understand, we gather pollen in its hypnosis. To place God's name naked on the street is to care little about its well-being. Man's psyche brings its name inside the ark to protect it from exposure, so it suffers in his vow to keep it silent.

"The ancient Hebrews worshipped at one time or another a great many different gods. In fact, the learned Encyclopædia Biblica and Bishop Colenso tell us that the Hebrews shipped precisely the gods of the people among whom they dwelt." Yet their scriptures have been edited so as to make it appear that from Genesis on they worshipped only two forms of deity, one called the Elohim - a band of gods like those of Greeks and Romans, and a special tribal god or Ba Al called IhOh or IhVh, whose name was too holy to permit of its being pronounced aloud; in fact, it was death to do so. The Scripture reader said Adonai instead." - James Ballantyne Hannay

* * *

Simeon the Just was Ba'alei Shem, or master of the name. The only priest to have access to the Tabernacle's inner tent. Around 300 BC, he emerged from the Holy of Holies, deeply saddened at the sight of a black apparition, and died several days later. From then on, the priests refrained from speaking or sharing the name of God in their priestly blessing.

God's name didn't die in a fire. It was smothered by a priesthood who thought its people weren't worthy of knowing how to say his name. An intricate bureaucracy developed around the keeping of the name. God's name became HaShem and Adonai. These were plastic coverings, or placeholders, incapable of suffering irreverence while the real name was locked away. An elaborate system of rituals and requirements went into the preservation and protection of the name of God. In his book, The Name, author Mark Sameth writes,

"The name is transmitted only to the reserved--this word can also be translated as "the initiate'-who are not prone to anger; who are humble and God-fearing, and carry out the commandments of their Creator. And it is transmitted only over water. Before the master teaches it to his pupil, they must both immerse themselves and bathe in forty measures of flowing water, then put on white garments and fast on the day of instruction. Then both must stand up to their ankles in the water, and the master must say a prayer ending with the words: 'The voice of God is over the waters! Praised be Thou, O Lord, who revealest Thy secret to those who fear Thee, He who knoweth the mysteries.' Then both must turn their eyes to the water and recite verses from the Psalms, praising God over the waters. "

The name YHWH is the name of God from the outside looking in. According to Jewish mystics, God's secret name is Hu-Hi which is the tetragrammaton unfolded. The sounds

Hu-Hi makes are the pronouns He-She combined, pointing to the androgyne, the Vitruvian man, as the ultimate sign of divinity.

The 13th Century Jew was telling the world it knew God's name, but it wasn't going to share it with anyone. It's a wonder they would ever feel persecuted. The Zohar recorded Rabbi Shimon's comments on sharing the name, "Woe is me if I speak! Woe is me if I do not speak!" Whether God's name be Api, Shamash, Tsur, Enlil, Nintud, El Elyon, IHOH, Elohim, Shaddai, Ehyeh, Adonia, HaShem, Kyrios, Dominus, Jehovah, Yahweh, Allah, Huwa, Baha, Shiva, Ptah, Nintud, Om, Ahura Mazda, Atum, Satnam, and even the sound of silence — man will kill to hide God's name as much as he did to spread it.

CHAPTER FIVE

Build, Flood, Repeat

All of us are carbon emissions. We are all green energy. We are all 100% recycled. Everything we do here is natural because we are nature. The environmental movement you see today is a post-traumatic stress reaction to a series of cataclysmic events that happened deep in our past. Governments and other opportunists will continue to capitalize on neurotic coping mechanisms to keep man distracted from what scares him; his mortality. But this realm is not the place to be clinging to permanence. Gaia will constantly move the furniture to keep the accommodations fresh for her guests. Like she says, "You don't have to go home. But you can't stay here."

The irony of the flood is all of that water breeds an epigenetic thirst for preservation. While in office, fundamentalists scolded Benjamin Netanyahu daily, insisting he wasn't working fast enough. "We're running out of time, Benny," they would say, or, "You're not doing enough" According to them, 217 years remain before time is up. Seeded into their religion is this 6,000-year limit before a divine force returns to wipe out what he created. The collective memory knows something, and it's encrypted in our mythology.

Geologists propose the possibility of a great flood in the Middle East about 6,600 years ago. At that time, the Black Sea was a freshwater lake surrounded by farmlands. It takes 25,800 years to complete one revolution of the equinoxes around the ecliptic. Randal Carlson believes the earth has experienced six resets in the last six of these Great Years. Randal calls them "potentially civilization-ending catastrophic events." In the last 150,000 years, that averages one reset every 15,000 years.

Half of these events happened on the cusp of Leo. Three on the entry into Aquarius, and the remaining two on the entrances into Scorpio and Taurus. These are the four stations of the Great Year's Cross. We can still see their bells ringing in the rocks. The last one rang in Leo 12,900 years ago, known as the Onset of the Younger Dryas. Before that, it was in Aquarius labeled the Onset of the Late Wisconsin Ice Age. Out of the last 150,000 years, we barely remember 6,000 of them. We have no idea what has been here before and how much of this place has been altered by man.

Years ago - Cusp - Cataclysm
   12,900 - Leo - Onset of Younger Dryas
   26,000 - Aquarius - Onset Late Wisconsin Ice Age
   39,000 - Leo - Heinrich Event 4
   52,000 - Aquarius - Heinrich Events OSIS 14, 15
   65,000 - Leo - Heinrich Event 6
   72,000 - Scorpio - Toba Super Eruption
   84,000 - Taurus - BP Odderade Event & Osis 21
   104,000 - Aquarius - Greenland Blitz
   117,000 - Leo - Terminal Substage 5E Climate Shift
   144,000 - Leo - Salian Climate Shift

The primitive mind stores the loss of advanced technology by encoding it as magic. It's the only way for the mythology to file the event. Tomorrow's software will become the jinn, or demons, of the ancient past. This ancient past can be referenced backward or forwards. Like the chicken and the egg, the past and present spawned each other. This is an important piece to remember when decrypting mythology.

"When God intended to create Adam he decided to punish human's predecessors. God obliterates the Nasnas [giants], and created a veil between jinn and humans" - Ali ibn Ibrahim

The proof is in the corn. Maize is unarguably an ancient genetic technology that predates primitive man. Books about genetically altered humans are no longer kept in the fiction section. We have been limited to a linear lens when studying our history, and so we have missed all of our footprints from the future buried in the past.

The Chinese have a version of Abraxas in the twin brother and sister, Fuxi and Nüwa. The twins bore the face of humans and the body of snakes. They are credited with populating the world after surviving a flood stuffed in a gourd. In Iran, Ahura Mazda advises Yima to construct an enclosure and populate it with two of every animal, bird, and plant and to supply it with light, food, and water. Flood mythology is corroborated all over the world. By the Choctaw, the Hopi, the Cherokee, the Incas, the Aztecs, and the Inuits. Same for Greece, China, Russia, Syria, Iran, Persia, and Italy. It's a long list, and the general themes give us insight into our collective unconscious experiences. Its plasma has been around longer than all of us, and our ancestral memory is inside its cloud.

The Tower of Babel and the flood story intermix. Both are recordings of ancient trauma where man seeks redemption. From sacrificial virgins to eating bugs, man insists he can stop a volcano with his behavior. It's like battered spouse syndrome with cataclysms. Man's collective unconscious is a budding child whose behavior seems atrocious outside this lens. But man's god is learning as we feed it.

A digital photograph with 100,000 pixels can be reduced to a few thousand thanks to JPEG compression. Without it, you wouldn't be able to keep those memories. This is how mythology works too. Mythology compresses history by finding its tiniest denominator. Once it does, the essence of the memory can be preserved while its details discarded. This technique allows information to be stored for thousands and thousands of years. It also causes stacking, where multiple memories sharing the same denominator write on the same page. Because of this, every deluge that's ever happened is stored as a single event.

Nimrod was the architect of the Tower of Babel, and Xelhua was the architect of the Mound of Cholula. Contrary to Nimrod's infamy, Xelhua's work still stands today and is the largest pyramid in the world by volume. Its name originates from the ancient Nahuatl, meaning "place of refuge." The part of southern Mexico was called the "place of refuge from water that falls." The flood myth and the tower myth are the same. Both constructions were preservers for mankind to survive a reset.

Before the great inundation 4,800 years after the erection of the world, the country of Anahuac was inhabited by giants. When the waters subsided, one of the giants, called Xelhua, surnamed the 'Architect,' went to Cholula, where, as a memorial of the Tlaloc which had served for an asylum to himself and his six brethren, he built an artificial hill in the form of a pyramid. The gods beheld, with wrath, this edifice the top of which was to reach the clouds. Irritated at his attempt, they hurled fire on his pyramid. - Ophiolatreia

* * *

The Hebrew word for tower in Babel's Tower is migdal. This word shares the same etymology as almond. So the tower could be understood as the almond of Babel. This connection is made significant by the contents of the Ark of the Covenant. The Rod of Aaron kept inside was the branch of a budding almond. The ark was a covenant or promise for preservation. Fertility is the symbol of everlasting life. The tower and the ark are one.

It wasn't an accident the Ark came to rest on Mount Ararat. This sacred mountain is still today known as Allah's Lat. The r's and l's are often intermingled through time. Allah's Lat was Arah's Rat which was written as Mount Ararat. The ark of preservation, or almond of babel, met the divine phallus, the Priapus, in a covenant to repopulate the earth. Noah was on the water for 284 days of human gestation.

The ark in the story of Gilgamesh was shaped like a box, not a boat. Utnapishtim's instructions for the ark resembled a cube 200 feet in each direction. Its plan called for seven floors, with its top floor housing the ark's fresh water. This design would be doomed the moment it floated. One of its features required the ability to block sunlight. Like the story of Ahura Mazda, the ark was designed to block light; as the text explains, "The Preserver of Life was made of solid timber so that the rays of Shamash (the sun) would not shine in." A gnostic text tells the story of Noah surviving the deluge in an ark of darkness where they remained sheltered within a luminous cloud.

It is not as Moses said, "He hid himself in an ark." but she sheltered him in a place, not Noah alone but men from the immovable race (giants). They went into a place and sheltered themselves with a luminous cloud. And he (Noah) recognized his lordship and those who were with him in the light which shone upon them, because darkness was falling over everything upon earth.

Measurements from the Old Testament's ark are as precise as they are seaworthy. The dimensions of 300 cubits by 50 cubits by 30 cubits are accurate because they came from the ships that were already sailing during the time of the story's dictation. Noah's flood was a later narrator's translation of the many deluge stories recorded before it. This is how all mythology is made.

Deucalion was saved from a deluge by building a chest, thanks to the urging of his father, Prometheus. Like the biblical Noah and the Mesopotamian counterpart Utnapishtim, he uses this device to survive the deluge with his wife, Pyrrha, daughter of Epimetheus. Epimetheus and Prometheus were creator twins whose children would repopulate the earth by throwing stones over their shoulders.

In Hindu teachings, Manu, the first man, was visited by Lord Vishnu, who told Manu the world would be destroyed in a great flood. Manu built a boat and tied it to the horn of the great fish. The fish guided Manu's ship through the floods and to the top of a mountain. Manu performed a ritual sacrifice when the floodwaters receded and poured butter and sour milk[3] into the sea. After a year, a woman rose from the water. Manu and his "daughter" then repopulate the earth.

In chapter 105 of the Book of Enoch, Methuselah, father of Lamech, grandfather of Noah, is told he would beget giants on the earth. He described them as "not spiritual, but carnal." Before these giants could be born, Methuselah was told of the great punishment that would be inflicted on them in the future. Punishing giants before they are born is a strategy, not

---

[3] Similar theme in the birth of Aphrodite, the castration of Uranus by Cronos, and the meaning of the name Titicaca's Viracocha.

punitive retribution. Methuselah is told about the nature of the carnal giants because that was their job. They were a starter pack designed to be reaped once they seeded the soil. Farmers call this technique a cover crop.

And all the others together with them took unto themselves wives, and each chose for himself one, and they began to go in unto them and to defile themselves with them, and they taught them charms, and enchantments, and the cutting of roots, and made them acquainted with plants. And they became pregnant. - The Book of Enoch, Chapter 7

Many giant myths incorporate the idea giants failed a moral test and were punished. But looking closely, you notice the giants were installing ancient wisdom into man. Methuselah is told all of these things will happen once the giants arrive,

"Afterwards shall greater impiety take place than that with had been before … Generation after generation shall transgress until a righteous race shall arise … Then the Lord will effect a new thing upon the earth."

If the Lord knew what an awful job he would do, why didn't he change his course from the beginning? The best answer here is that the giants were made that way for a purpose. God does the same thing to Adam's son, Cain, by shunning his offering as a farmer. God's curse on Cain was breaking his stalk so he, like the giants, would thrive. Noah would use the same technique on his offspring, Canaan. In horticulture, this is notching. The method recruits the flow of hormones around the wound to stimulate rapid growth. The idea that God saw humanity as evil or broken contradicts his invitation for a few of its members to persist and spread their genes into a new crop. If the goal is to remove every human, saving one or two would be a colossal waste of water. Every flood story has an underlying theme of human preservation. It seems to be the entire purpose of the deluge process. If it weren't, we probably wouldn't be remembering them, now would we?

The flood is the obliteration of memory, not life. You remember nothing when you are born. The only memory you have is water. Genesis is a flood. The first thing we do is separate ourselves from its water. Memory is the separation from amnesia. To remember is to emerge. This is the meaning of day one in the Bible. Day one is the creation of memory. Ka is at the root of every memory because memories are built from an origin, and man's origin is a flood.

One of the oldest constellations in the sky sank to the bottom of memory to be forgotten. The Argo Navis was called the Ark of the Milky Way. Man no longer needs the Ark, so its timbers can be repurposed in the psyche. Each constellation is a ladder, and humanity will use every rung he can find. The constellation Corvus is the blackbird. The constellation Columba is the white dove. Both were sent out of the ark to find land. Only Columba, the dove, returns. The rising of Corvus always marked the beginning of the rainy season, not the end. Therefore, Corvus could not return. These three constellations have sailed the equatorial since the first memories were formed. The flood was a beginning as much as it was an end.

CHAPTER SIX

Rise of Priapus

Before words, there was the gesture. Man's ability to point at something across the field so that others understand him took a long time to develop. Have you ever tried pointing at a piece of cheese to a dog? The good boy is insistent all of the action lies on your finger. Grasping the meaning of each other's gestures is a mastery of our mammalian brain. The gesture is the fundamental foundation used by all words to transmit meaning. When you dissect them, every letter in every word is just a tiny gesture made by the tongue or the pen.

The Yarek Oath is a gesture of swearing on the phallus. It was cleaned up for primetime audiences in the Bible.

So the servant put his hand under the thigh of his master Abraham and swore an oath to him concerning this matter. - Genesis 24:9

In Rome, castrated genitals were used as divining instruments in court. Megalithic stones shaped like the phallus were commissioned as truth rocks where vows were made and witnessed. The phallus was a source of righteousness and truth long before it was shamed and circumcised.

He called for his son Joseph and said to him, "put your hand under my thigh and promise that you will show me kindness and faithfulness. Do not bury me in Egypt" - Genesis 47:29

You're probably not going to find a lot of lesbians in Roman archeology. At least not the kind who sees the penis as repulsive. The ones that do remain in archeology are either really dedicated or downright masochistic. Imagine spending years huddled in an ancient latrine in Italy, cataloging thousands of ceremonial phalluses and stroking each of them meticulously with a brush. Religion came riding into town on a sacred dildo, and Rome has the proof in its gutter. In 1786, Richard Payne Knight penned his essay, The Worship of Priapus. This excerpt from the publisher's preface a hundred years later explains its publication's delay.

The bold utterances of Mr. Knight on a subject which until that time had been entirely tabooed, or had been treated in a way to hide rather than to discover the truth, shocked the sensibilities of the higher classes of English society, and the ministers and members of the various denominations of the Christian world. Rather than endure the storm of criticism, aroused by the publication, he suppressed during his lifetime all the copies of the book he could recall, consequently it became very scarce, and continued so for nearly a hundred years.

And Knight wasn't even breaking new ground. He was building off the archeological work of Mr. D'Hancarville, who had documented thousands of sacred dildos in various styles and mediums that Knight referenced in his work. Knight was presenting the litany of evidence for the worship of Priapus. It was suppressed for a hundred years and tainted Knight's career in Parliament. His book is still labeled as pornography today. It becomes impossible to study religion holistically when we sweep so much of it under the table. But the worship of Priapus was the worship of creation, and it wasn't a pagan orgy. Admittedly, some of it included pagan orgies, but it was also a religion. Knight explains, "The initiated were obliged to purify themselves by abstaining from venery and all impure food."

In Plate 1 of his work, he presents a collection of wax phalluses typical of the many offered to the Church of Isernia. Plate 2 is an illustrated bust of a man with a rooster's head and a penis snout with the greek inscription "Savior of the World" underneath. Plate 9 features a dual-gendered Apollo in repose. Plate 26 features a spry-looking parrot phallus with another phallus emerging from his shoulder. Petey is seated on a stump of vaginas in the shape of a bouquet. I promise what I am describing isn't pornography. These are archeological sketches of artifacts found in Rome on excavations. Knight shows the variety and proliferation of phallic relics from the past. Some had appendages, some were on chains, and some were shaped like birds. Hundreds of phallic fidget spinners have been found in every corner of Rome. They all show a rise of a divine erection in the collective psyche. Are they lewd? Of course. Lewd is what gave them power. They are still glowing today with the prana of early man. It is tangible in the shame felt when we look at them now. The Priapus was the eternal begetter and the self-illumined. He is the Father of Night because he creates the desire for light to shine. He is the lucid splendor of creation and generation, active and passive, male and female.

Among the remains of Roman civilization in Gaul, we find statues or statuettes of Priapus, altars dedicated to him, the gardens and fields entrusted to his care, and the phallus, or male member, figured in a variety of shapes as a protecting power against evil influences of various kinds. With this idea the well-known figure was sculptured on the walls of public buildings, placed in conspicuous places in the interior of the house, worn as an ornament by women, and suspended as an amulet to the necks of children. Erotic scenes of the most extravagant description covered vessels of metal, earthenware, and glass, intended, no doubt, for festivals and usages more or less connected with the worship of the principle of fecundity. - Richard Payne Knight

As a creator, Priapus was in the business of fertility. He was a hard habit for Christians to break. The Lanercost Chronicle reports in the year 1268, a pestilence prevailed in the Scottish district of Lothian, which was fatal to the cattle. Some clergy told the people to "build a need-fire and raise up the image of Priapus." In 1282, a parish priest performed the rites of Priapus by making the young children dance round a pole as he urged them on with a wooden phallus. Scorned by the bishop, the priest defended himself, saying it was a country tradition.

The placing of a phallus on walls and doors prevailed into the middle ages. Churches were tagged the most with these decals despite the clergy's protest. It was too late. The divine boner was erect in the psyche. Not to be outdone or ignored, the Priapus had its counterpart in the vulva. The female organ was a protector of the church and featured in gaping prominence on the keystones above church doorways.

In Provence, France, waxen images of genitalia offered to St. Foutin were suspended from the chapel's ceiling. When the wind blew, it "very much disturbs the devotions of the worshippers." In nearby Embrun, the phallus of St. Foutin is bathed in wine, and the juice is bottled as holy vinegar. When the Protestants took the village, they found the large phallus among the relics; its head was still stained red.

A sizeable wooden phallus is scraped by the fingernails of barren women and made into a tea to spur virility and fertility. A large phallus covered in leather is worshipped at St. Eutropius, but the Protestants burnt the idol in a ceremony in 1562. In nuptial ceremonies, the bride would offer her virginity to Priapus by rubbing her genitals against him. A few of these gatherings made it into the pages of the Bible.

You also took the fine jewelry I gave you, the jewelry made of my gold and silver, and you made for yourself male idols and engaged in prostitution with them. - Ezekiel 16:17

The Festival of Liberalia dates back to Rome. Every March, a monstrous phallus was carried in procession while followers indulged in obscene songs and revelry, ending when a queen ceremoniously crowned the head of the phallus with garland. As in the Floralia, the arrival of the festival was announced by the sounding of horns the previous evening. No sooner had midnight arrived than the youth of both sexes proceeded in couples to the woods to gather branches and make garlands which they were to return just at sunrise to decorate the doors of their houses.

When the flute stirs, the loins and the [roadies] of Priapus sweep along, frenzied alike by the horn-blowing and the wine, whirling their locks and howling. What foul longings burn within their breasts! What cries they utter as the passion palpitates within! How drenched their limbs in torrents of old wine! ... And now impatient nature can wait no longer; woman shows herself as she is, and the cry comes from every corner of the den, "Let in the men!" - The Satires of Juvenal

St. Augustine wrote about Liberalia in detail. He documented every step of the phallus parade and the ceremony of its crowning. He called it "a most obscene figure done to appease the god, and to obtain an abundant harvest, and remove enchantments from the land." Every spring, the Priapus resurrected from the ground as the Maypole. The sixteenth-century Puritan writer Philip Stubbes reported from one of the events sounding like a war correspondent clutching his pearls.

"Every Maie, Every parish, town, and village assembles themselves together, both men, women, and children, old and young, they go out into the woods and groves where they spend all night in pleasantries. But their cheerest jewell they bring home is their Maie pole. They have twenty or forty yoke of oxen, every oxe having a sweet bouquet of flowers placed on the tip of his horns as they draw home their pole with two or three hundred men, women, and children following it with great devotion. And thus they rear it up, with handkerchiefs and flags and streamers on the top, and straw the ground about it placing greene boughs all about it. And they banquet and feast, and leap and dance about it, as the heathen people did."

How does Christianity compete with an ancient Maypole fertility ritual? Like the rooster at dawn, the Priapus rises and falls regardless of anyone's objections. The Puritan Stubbes was flustered, saying, "Out of a hundred maidens who go out to the woods that night, there are scarcely a third returned home again undefiled."

One of the oldest rituals in Greece is the oiling of the phallus, where virgins would come out of the temple at dusk to stroke a giant wooden pillar in the center of the garden with virgin-pressed olive oil. Erections, ecstasy, and even ejaculation were vital parts of the religious experience before the idea of God decided to wear pants.

Probably the most famous divine erection was Osiris.

Plutarch traced the phallus of Osiris to the Bacchus of Greek Mythology. Osiris was chopped into fourteen pieces, and all were recovered except his priapus. This was the turning point for the worship of Min when the erection morphed into a cross. The cross is the sword inverted. It represents control of the erection. Just as discretion is a sign of power, so too is abstinence a sign of virility. The sacred whore became the sacred virgin.

The word of the Lord came to me: "What do you see, Jeremiah?"
"I see the branch of an almond tree," I replied. - Jeremiah 1:11

The almond is one of the oldest references to the clitoris. Temple women, or sacred harlots, were called "Migdalenes" or "Magdalenes." The name Mary Magdalene was a professional title. She was a temple prostitute or an "almond" woman of the temple. In biblical times, the Kadeshoth, or dedicated women, were attached in great numbers to all temples. They were the source of the temple's revenue and draw. James Ballantyne Hannay dissects The Book of Samuel Chapters 5 and 6, explaining the Ark was a thermonuclear STD device. It's the best explanation I've heard for the meaning of the story of the five golden "Emerods."

The passage means taking the sexual use of the Hebrew women to grace the Philistines' temple brothels. In consequence, they took "Ophalim in their secret parts" (man-woman disease disguised as "Emerods"), meaning a double-sex disease (O woman, Phallim male organs), or syphilis. The Philistines made five golden" Emerods," models of the combined sex organs, and five golden mice (male organs, "little secret things of the night") purely phallic emblems. So the double-sex disease, syphilis, was cured by golden images of the organs involved in sacred prostitution. - James Ballantyne Hannay

* * *

So many sexual rites have been censored from scripture. This is why the Priapus is so important to understand the context of the scripture. In verse 9, most translations leave out the part explaining that the tumor outbreak was specific to the groin, which means those weren't tumors.

"But after they had moved it, the Lord's hand was against that city, throwing it into a great panic. He afflicted the people of the city, both young and old, with an outbreak of tumors (in the groin)" - 1 Samuel 5:9

Over thousands of years, significant parts of the scripture are lost, censored, reinterpreted, and finally denied were ever there. I wouldn't be the first to say this verse probably had to do with syphilis.

"and followed the Israelite into the tent. He drove the spear into both of them, right through the Israelite man and into the woman's stomach. Then the plague against the Israelites was stopped;" - Numbers 25:8

We are witnessing ancient history dissolve one letter at a time.

Egyptian has only one sign for R and L, and unfortunately the first readers of the hieroglyphics chose the wrong letter, as the kingly title of Egypt is one of these double-sex names, from the male Pala of India coupled with the female ring or oval 0; so the name should be Phala - O, or Phala - Oh, not Phara - oh, as we write it, and certainly not Fair - oh, as we pronounce it. So the "Fairo," as we call the Egyptian ruler, should be Pala - o or Phala - o, not Phara - oh, and it is so written on the monuments. In Greece "pala" became "phallos," and in Latin "phallus," from which we derive the adjective "phallic," used to describe all literature. - James Ballantyne Hannay, The Rise, Decline And Fall Of The Roman Religion

Hannay explains that the Egyptian hieroglyphs show ka represented as the phallus. The Pharaoh Ka Kau, therefore was know as Phallus, son of the Phallus. This is like being named Penis Penison, or Dick son of Dick. Don't laugh, Priapus was serious work. This was man's teenage psyche dreaming about girls. It used to be normal to have an anti-modest ritual uncorked every moon cycle in town. These were times to exhale when "all bonds were loosed." Making this happen required a parade with a salaciously large model of a phallus. Success would see the event end in a mosh pit of wanton abandon and the phallus delivered. New Orleans keeps the Priapus alive as best it can.

At the celebration of Floralia, Cato, not at all disapproving of the licentious exhibitions, retired, so that his well-known gravity or modesty might in no wise restrain the celebrants, because the multitude showed hesitation in stripping the "nuns" or sacred prostitutes stark - naked in presence of a man so celebrated for his modesty. - James Ballantyne Hannay

Man's ability to hold a trance in public was a budding skill, and pretending to be civilized could be tiresome. These festivities were more than necessary; they were required for social stability. Their names paint a picture of the human spirit desperate to be relieved from the pressure of holding its act together: Liberalia, Floralia, Lupercalia, Vulcanalia, Fornicalia, Bacchanalia, Dionysiaca Maternalia, Hilaria, Priapeia, Bona Dea, and Adonai. A shaman would see these festivals as medicine for the animal in man. The Heyoka, or sacred clowns, of the southwest, knew how to release tension in the village. You can picture these kinds of rituals naturally springing up all over the world. Man is not static. He is forever reaching. This is the very essence of erection.

The counting of moons told them it was spring, and the stars agreed. Every fire in the village had been extinguished for days, and every hearthstone was raised. Men painted in black wrapped themselves in wolfskins and formed a circle at the village's heart. They tied their feet to giant drums and began to blow their giant horns. The sound bellowed and shook every house until it was awake. Every man and woman emerged from their huts and retreated into the forest, whooping and yipping. Their clothing fell like breadcrumbs as each villager morphed back into something primitive. All night they would squeeze the earth with their toes while their fingers gathered moss, boughs, and flowers for the dawn's rising. They sang songs without words and touched each other as if no one had names anymore. Gathering mandrake, charged with tender kisses, each of them was a child again in the time before the fire. As the horns pushed them further into the wild, all they could be was alive.

The Egyptian Ankh symbolizes everlasting life split between two worlds on a horizon. The "O" is the vulva above the "I," the phallus. The Ankh's intersection manifests the Horus Son, the horizon of the two. This is the everlasting life in the Ankh. It is invoked in marriage when the wedding ring is placed around a finger. It is seen in the joining of "I" and "O" in the Greek Phi. The Ankh is the mortise and its tenon, the Lingham and its Yoni, the male and female of Vitruvian Man.

The Omphalos is a historical megalithic stone at the Temple of Delphi, said to be the navel of the world. Two eagles flew opposite directions to measure the center of the world and came to meet at the Omphalos. This was the home of the Oracle at Delphi. For a thousand years, it was the center of the world. The joining of Om and Phalos is the Ankh. The rock at Delphi people kiss, and stroke for luck is not a magic belly button. It is the Phalos or the Priapus.

The National Library in Paris has a collection of Abbey Tokens believed to be given to "frequenters of the sacraments." Abbey tokens were used widely in England, Scotland, and Ireland. Romish Churches still present these tokens on the first communion. Until the 17th century, the official liturgy of the Church of Scotland stated, "So many as intend to be partakers of the Holy Communion shall receive Tokens from the minister the night before."

"On the edge, it reads Bibite Cum Laetitia, Drink ye with gladness. Its origin may be more properly civil than sacramental, though the words on the rim are virtually what I have heard a hundred times at the communion table in Scotland, "Eat, O friends; drink, yea, drink abundantly, O beloved." - The Story of the Token by Robert Shiells.

The phrases on these tokens seen through the unwashed eye of Priapus translates the early meanings of the phrase "Salvation by St. Peter" and "Love one Another." The power of the cloth was the ancient power of the pimp. The church wouldn't have been invented without it. There is evidence of jealousy and competition between the different orders of the clergy as to whose tokens should be admitted for communion with one of the abbey's virgins. As the church grew more discrete in the shaming of Priapus, these tokens eventually became oath keepers. Groups like the Rosicrucians were able to tokenize church secrets, turning them into an underground economy.

In church, a sermon is delivered from the pulpit. The word pulpit is the male and the female sex organs combined. The Ankh separated into its parts are the monstrance and the pyx.

These are Catholic ritual props encoding the sacred genitals. The monstrance is a decorated vulva, and the pyx is the seed of Priapus. The implements are carried in a procession at the opening of the service to signify the foreplay. The climax becomes the service where they meet.

The punishment of death was meted out also to anyone touching, looking into or inquiring as to our monstrance and pyx — the monstrance being an "almond" -shaped or dove - shaped vessel representing woman, or the membrum femininum, and the pyx a rod - like article which lay inside the monstrance (or mother), and death was meted out to one of our soldiers by his being hanged, drawn and quartered in sight of the French enemy (for having touched the monstrance and pyx) before the battle of Agincourt. - James Ballantyne Hannay

God rose from the waters of the collective unconscious through the phallus to Abraxas into Pan. Capricorn is a goat-headed Abraxas called Aegipan, the tropic between fish and man. The plasma of man's belief is strongest in the sea. The salt of Sheol is mythology's power source and antenna. Inside man's mind, God can cut the cord restricting him to the coast. Aegipan was the incestuous child of Valerius and his daughter Valeria which shows the dedication giants paid to their carnal calling. Their era was not the time to be concerned with who fathered who. Aegipan was shameless and often seen as Satyr, the hoofed man-horse who brandished his erection in public like a hood ornament. Unlike the Biblical accounts painting the giants as having genetic defects, Aegipan helps mankind evolve. Working with Hermes, Aegipan helps Zeus overcome Typhon, the hundred-headed child born from the rage of Hera. Hera was angry at Zeus for self-spawning a child without her, so she self-spawned a child without him and called it Typhon, her

100-headed avenger. As you can tell, hypocrisy was not on the radar back then; people were too busy playing with their Priapus.

CHAPTER SEVEN

Divine Twins

Priapus begets duality. From the one sprang two — from the two sprang all. The divine twins appear in the Nile as Hapi, the fertility deity. Known as the father of the gods, Hapi features ripe blue breasts and a ceremonial beard. The Hapi twins are hermaphroditic self-creators who spawn all life. The duo unites the papyrus and the lotus in a symbol called the Sema Tawy. The Sema Tawy is a transatlantic icon found in Europe and the Americas showing a mythological placeholder linking the hermaphroditic twins with creation.

The Iroquois had creator twins, and the Mayans did, too. Heracles and Iphicles were twins, as were Castor and Pollux. The Christos and the Kristna are twins. Twins were the founding rulers of Sparta, and their successors would be twins by decree. The coat of arms of Russia is a double-headed eagle bearing a scepter decorated with another double-headed eagle. Twins giving birth to twins are everywhere in mythology.

The twelve Titans were incestuous twins, one male, and one female, each the other's reproductive partner. They hatched children from their severed appendages. They were primordial spawning farms with little regard for themselves or what happened to their children. The Titans Oceanus and Tethys were so fertile they had to get a divorce to save the world. Despite being brother and sister, Hyperion and Theia birthed the sun, moon, and dawn. The wonder twins Cronus and Rhea were fertile but were caught eating most of their children. The siblings Conus and Phoebe gave birth to Apollo, who's twin was Artemis.

The Titans tell us the story of the zygote, the young single-celled Priapus invoking the ancient ritual of the divine twin. He speaks the spell's vibration four times, carving the zodiac's cross into his vaulted trophoblast. This process is known as cell cleavage. The one becomes two, the two become four, the four become eight, and the eight becomes sixteen—four twins in four cardinal directions. Cell cleavage is different from the typical cell reproduction of mitosis. Like the Titans, cell cleavage is incestuous and cannibalistic. None of its twins produce growth. Instead, each parent cuts itself in half to make its twin. That's how it works in an ark — more lives are on board, but the square footage remains the same. The incest and the cannibalism of the Titans were necessary for survival on a voyage through Fallopian's tube.

After the ark touched the ground on the side of Mount Uterus, a new life began. Gone are the incest and cannibalism of cell cleavage. The zygote is a blastocyst now and mitosis can utter its new testament. The Titans forge a massive firmament around their new kingdom, and the ka sets root in the mud of the womb. The ark's seal is opened, and the city's canals flood with water for the first time. The Titan siblings Mnemosyne and Themis gave birth to memory. We see them in the production of sodium when water penetrates the blastocyst's walls. The sodium produced in this deluge provides a blastocyst with the ability to store its first memory in salt. The lifeform has memories now — its kingdom is its own personal Sheol.

This is why the Book of Genesis says God created the heavens and the earth but not the water. The water was already here in the womb. The Titan story is a play-by-play of biology, not mythology. We see the Tower of Babel fall inside the blastocyst when all of its cells are differentiated into two poles. This process is portrayed when the Titans, Crius, and Iapetus, hold down their father, Uranus so that Cronos can castrate him. This separation into poles is the birth of gender inside the organism's kingdom. The Titan's cells were androgynous before the fall. It is astounding how much the writers of ancient mythology resonated with the reproductive process sans ultrasound or microscope.

The male's sperm and the female's egg are the only cells in your body that are missing a pair of genes. This is what attracts them to each other. They are desperately naked in the world, looking for their twin flame. The magic of sex is a union of the cleaved. It puts out so much energy a new life is born from its chamber. And when finally combined, the first thing they do in union is separate, and that separation is life. Life is the one-ing of two and the two-ing of one over and over and over again.

CHAPTER EIGHT

Eye of Horus

Archeology calls them "intrusive burials," which muddies the water. But like the lotus, truth doesn't mind the mud. The tombs in the valley were holes for the planted placenta; these were communal shrines. The grooves are still in the rock where wooden doors would slide. You don't put a wooden door on a stone tomb and call it a secret. The phenomenon of turning every hole into a private cemetery is a new invention of the occupiers of previous antiquity.

Man is a twin like the lotus. His other is the falcon in the sky. Place your palms flat, fingers together, extend your arms like wings, and bend the elbows to form the symbol for ka. This gesture amplifies the antenna. Prayer sends, but ka receives. You do not pray to Horus; you receive him. Right now, a royal cord is plugged into your belly, connecting you both. Horus is your eye in the sky. All of us have Horus. Horus is the organ who died to bring us through the underworld. Horus is placenta. Your placenta has always watched over his king. You are his lotus, Osiris. You are not wounded; you are cleaved.

The Ganda people call the placenta a second child, Mulongo, who is born dead. His ghost is intimately connected to the welfare of the newborn. The placenta is a genius, and linking to it makes a man's oracles highly accurate. In Egypt, the moon god, Khons, is the Pharaoh's placenta dressed in the likeness of a young prince. The placenta was vital to ka. So was the cord. On the West Bank of Luxor, Tomb TT3 features a painting depicting Osiris, Horus, and the Valley of the Gates. Horus is at the base of the valley as if inside it. His offering of incense to Osiris symbolizes the spirit of ka sent from the mountain to Osiris. This single painting captures the essence and spirit of Karnak and the Vitruvian Adam.

Horus is associated with funeral offerings because the placenta dies at birth. Horus struggles with Set in the underworld of the womb and gives his eye so that Osiris may survive. The side, or rib, of Vitruvian Adam that is cleaved becomes the placenta. An umbilical cord connects the twins. Horus, the placenta, calls the birth of Osiris the afterlife because Horus dies when his king is delivered. The symbolism of Horus losing an eye to save Osiris is one twin forgoing muscles and organs so that another may be born. In many versions of the story, Osiris consumes the eye of Horus. Horus is the eye of the moon because the moon doesn't burn; it glows. Horus will never be alive on the surface to see Ra. Like the falcon in the sky, Horus is everywhere. The Horus-scope is your eye in the sky. You consult it to divine what's best for you. You will pay attention to its intuition because it earned your trust a long time ago.

Thoth plays an important role here as Lady Justice. Thoth will decide the baby's fate by declaring a truce between Set and Horus. The truce has dire consequences, though, because only one of the twins may live. Horus is therefore sentenced to die by Thoth in exchange for Osiris being born. This is the origin story of one man dying so another may live. It goes all the way back to Egypt.

The tradition of burying the placenta in sacred soil is fused with Horus when his mother Isis waters his injured eye with milk and grape vines grow. Egypt is the body. The underworld is the womb. The twin that never grows an eye is the Horus. He is the eye in the sky because the placenta sits above the baby. Set is hunger, neglect, miscarriage, and exposure.

"And they say to Osiris: You went away, you have returned. You woke, you fell asleep. You are enduring in life. Arise! Behold this! Arise! Hear this, what your son has done for you! What Horus has done for you!'" - Pyramid Texts, utterance 482

In the Papyrus," The Contendings of Horus and Seth," the two compete in a trial before a nine-member council symbolic of the nine-month pregnancy. During the trial, Horus is constantly challenged by Set and never loses, as in the baby doesn't die. When Horus is finally named victorious, Osiris is born. You can see why an Egyptian would focus on Horus during birth. You can also see why Horus is always associated with death. We only get to see Horus alive in the underworld, in our womb. This Papyrus has a lot of sex juice and genital mutilation text eluding to the birth of fertility when the Vitruvian Adam was cleaved.

"Once a month the Twin was carried into the royal presence, and placed before the king, who took it out of its wrappings of bark cloth and inspected it. This was done at each new moon; and had to be exposed in the doorway of the temple for the moon to shineupon it."
- The Baganda, p. 236

The doorway mentioned is the same concept that led to the naming of the Valley of the Gates of Kings. The Pharaohs Neter-Khet and Menkau-Ra buried their placentas in dedicated tombs just as lavish and massive as their own burial chambers. The Hopi Indians keep the placenta for twenty days until the child is given its name. In Japan, the placenta is buried in cedar wood beneath the house. In 1418, North Korean Sejong the Great had his placenta enshrined in a tomb open to tourists. When a Mayan child is born, the placenta is buried in the ground as a religious ritual. This place holds special meaning for the Maya; it is where the individual is symbolically "planted" in the ground to root their Mayan identity. The placenta is called the "bundle of life" in the Bible twice.

Yet a man is risen to pursue thee, and to seek thy soul: yet the soul of my lord shall be bound in the bundle of life with the Lord thy God - 1 Samuel 25:29

Egyptologist Margaret Murray explained when the king became old, ritual murder was common. During this rite, the "bundle of life" containing the royal placenta was opened and resealed as a sign of reverence to Horus.

CHAPTER NINE

The Sword in the Stone

Thrust your sword into the stone, and its hilt becomes a planted cross. The Sovereign's Orb is one of the Crown Jewels and embodies this image. It is the ancient symbol for iron in alchemy. The Lady of the Lake is the heart, and her name is Viviane. She forges the sword Excalibur in her waters and gives it to her king. Its blade is sheathed in the stone of hemoglobin. The king releases Excalibur with every calorie he evaporates. King Author is the story of the body.

In many ancient villages, the lude place to go was church. Naves were often decorated with gaping vaginas. Stone pavers out front where you shake hands with the reverend were carved with scrotums. And why not? The roots of religion are the roots of creation, and sex is a motorcycle to eternity. No wonder it feels so good to be in that seat. But time unfurls, and mankind develops discretion. Swords are sheathed as mating rituals incorporate the strutting of reservation.

Over time sex symbols were removed from the church. Priapus became Pious. The penis was inverted and converted to Christianity. But the genitals remained under the cloak of this facelift. Look inside the Ark of the Covenant. The male is the rod and two stones. The female is the golden box that holds them. Moses placed the rod and its stones in the ark to preserve the covenant. The three-in-one God symbolized fertility and eternity because these things are the same. There are thirteen Egyptian obelisks in Rome spurting crosses from their tips to prove it. The trinity sprang forth from Priapus. Plutarch commented on the rise of the triple phallus amulet as one "carried in great favor" by the people. The same trinity organ as the fleur-de-lys.

A traditional Yiddish worshipper wears a shuckling around his waist to separate the heart from the genitals. The theory is during prayer; one must isolate the lower energies. Priapus was condemned to a cage of modesty, requiring him to dig his way out. Priapus can be seen at the wailing wall while its young men undulate emphatically. There was a time when worship and sex were the same. Young couples in love know this now. Ecstasy is a compass to God. All of the energy of worship emerges from an urge. The act of prayer is an erection of our reverence for the divine.

Moses had intercourse with the Shekhinah. - The Zohar

You can't turn worship off like a faucet. Every conscious thought is the worship of something. Everything you look at, think about, listen to, and do is worship. Everything you fight to ignore is worship. No one alive can turn worship off. Christianity would have no choice but to swallow his own Priapus.

As they were going up the hill to the town, they met some young women coming out to draw water, and they asked them, "Is the seer here?" "He is," they answered. "He's ahead of you. Hurry now; he has just come to our town today, for the people have a sacrifice at the high place." - 1 Samuel 9:11-12

* * *

This verse is meaningless to someone who doesn't know Priapus. The earliest temples were brothels; they didn't function on piety but cleanliness. The history of the nun dates back to the fish when a nunnery, a brothel, would lay fallow for a month to restore its virginity. If the sun rose in the house of Pisces, the brothel was closed. Their motto was, "cloistered nuns don't have syphilis." The verse from the Book of Samuel is the parable of Jack and Jill.

Jack and Gill went up the hill to fetch a pail of water. Jack fell down and broke his crown and Gill came tumbling after.

Going up the hill for water is counterintuitive because water is found at the bottom of hills. The "water atop the hill" means the brothel, the first church. And the verse was originally Jack and Gill, and their adventure up the hill got them syphilis. The piety of Christianity was spurred by two very important reasons. Firstly, it was a necessary eugenics program for a bloated population living the consequences of sanctioned monthly orgies on the street. The second reason was the rise of urbanized syphilis. The most successful temples were the ones with the cleanest virgins. A vestal virgin who lost her virginity would be punished with death, often by being buried alive. Patrons would pilgrimage for thousands of miles to the Parthenon because of the quality of its temple virgins. It was the same at Delphi. Imagine telling your spouse, "Hey. I'm going to Delphi to consult a temple virgin."

While Rome taxed, Judaism circumcised, and Christianity embraced both. Slavery is an instrument of growth. The ICHTHYS sigil was the eight-sided wheel encoding the names of Jesus, Christ, God, Son, and Savior all in one. Living by the redemption of a Savior is a posture of slavery.

Christianity was a medicine for struggle. Man holds a stigma around these tools which causes shame. But even his shame of slavery is growth. It shows how much he yearns to grow past it. Priapus is still there under the cloak. Every shameful erection made us grow.

The name IesU, our Jesus, is a combination of Roman and Indian symbolism. The I and U are Jupiter and Juno. The "es" is the union of the two in flesh. The great god of India were all double-sexed, like IHOH and IesU. Every symbol for the name of God are unions of male and female. As they should be. - James Ballantyne Hannay

Christ and Kristna are twins. In India, there was Christ + Na. In Rome, there was Christ + Os. Here's a compiled list of the multitude of similarities between them. Both were deities in the flesh from a virgin birth. Both were born poor but given expensive gifts. Both were born away from home due to required government errands. Both saw star-powered directional markers with pleasing sky sounds. Both had a lot of shepherds on the guest list. Both were preceded by mentors who were almost murdered. Both were well-learned when they were young. Both cured leprosy. Both declined an offer from the Devil to merge forces. Both were anointed by a poor woman who was probably a prostitute. Both performed a significant catering miracle with no notice or budget. Both walked upon the water. Both predicted their death. Both were pierced by metal. Both died and rose again. Both were fated to return on a white horse. Other than that, these are two completely different.

Egypt had a Christ called Serapis. He was a combination of Osiris and Apis, the bull god. Serapis welded Greek and Egypt in the flesh under a state-sponsored manly icon. Unlike Osiris, Serapis was alive and took Osiris' place next to Isis. His largest temple was the Serapeum in Alexandria, which serviced its great library. The temple was closed in 325 AD under the rule of Constantine. Six decades later, the Christians would destroy the Serapeum and all its contents in a mob. Symbolically, this was the last pagan stronghold. One of the most impressive structures in history was sacked and destroyed by a need for more repression and the dominance of a singular faith.

According to Eunapius, a pagan historian, the remains of criminals and slaves, who had been occupying the Serapeum at the time of the attack, were appropriated by Christians, placed in (surviving) pagan temples, and venerated as martyrs.

The Library of Alexandria was the first internet. Once Christianity took over the facility, it was cleansed and censored of pagan and curated scripture. You can see this clearly with a reading of Romans 13, when God calls for government obedience as his divine office. God was getting bigger than a church. Government is the progression of God's evolution into man's consciousness. Like a serpent, his plasma moves from Priapus to Abraxas to Serapis to Christos to Emperor to Pope. The name Joseph comes from the union of "IO" and "Seph." Seph is the serpent or the phallus.

In the age of Building 7, it should be easy to believe the burning of Rome was a controlled demolition. There was no upside to Nero saving Rome. It was a bloated republic with herpes, and a lot of people must have liked the idea of starting over. Etiquette tells you it was a tragedy when Rome burned, and truth tells you it was arson. But everyone knows lamp oil doesn't melt marble beams.

A funny thing happened on the way to the Holy War. The feminine parts of God were left at home. Four out of five soldiers prefer the phallus to the vulva as a symbol of intimidation on the battlefield. Man was growing and needed to kill people who disagreed. War demanded we deny the Shekinah in public. And so we slowly forgot. Every Holy War has been a battle for the collective unconscious to agree. This kind of quickening is built into any unitarian deity. The law of only one has consequences, and it has benefits. But the horsepower from a universal belief can feel like a dynamo of free energy to the one who shares the belief. It's surfing a monster wave.

I have blessed you by Yahweh of Samaria and his Asherah - Chimeric pole prayer

Yahweh's divorce from Asherah would be life-changing. Man's mind went from "4000 phalluses found in a roman orgy pit" to "The Lord is my Shepherd I shall not want." The Maypole flipped, and Peter's church would become a BDSM dungeon of martyrdom. The collective unconscious was rejecting its shadow, and the plasma was too much for a budding deity to behold. And so God, the collective unconscious, would become jealous and vengeful.

Fear is the body's way of rejecting power that's too intimidating. As the spirit of man gained energy, so did his attempts to shed it. This rejection shows itself in rituals like animal sacrifice, where the participant dumps a load of energy to make himself feel better. The medicine he employs requires an abrupt loss. Imagine coming home to find your neighbor who shot his family pet because he messed up at work. Would you remain his neighbor? The entire block of mankind had been acting like this for a long time. That kind of psychology only comes from someone who can't handle being wrong.

These are symptoms of weak ego. Until it has more capacity, it will need a way to offload the excess charge. This is the purpose of animal sacrifice and the ritual of the scapegoat. The collective unconscious was as violent and psychopathic as Yahweh was jealous and vengeful. Yahweh is the collective unconscious. They are the same being. The same entity. And it is growing with man. It is a living God because man's collective unconscious is a living plasma.

In mid-century France, this energy was managed through vaulderie. Vaulderie ran off the plasma of placebo whereby practitioners would exchange beliefs in the form of roots, rituals, and potions charged under a communal Sabbath. It has the essence of each other's witness in its vile, which makes its spell more potent. Women placed an anointed wood branch against their genitals and followed its pulse wherever it took them. Riding the broom was a dowsing rod to flow-state. It allowed the witch to enter her lower self, and it felt like flying when she found a vein. These Sabbaths were the continued worship of Priapus long after Rome was gone. They were liberations from the staunch fear instilled in a township violently insisting on civilization. A village requires the sacrifice of people to survive. The wrong person would lose a mule, and five weeks later, the burnt corpse of a dead witch is hanging at the crossroads. The individual will always be the weakest enemy of the mob. People forget the American colonists had violently enforced dress codes and rules for behavior. It didn't take much to be labeled a demon and suffer the scapegoat wrath of misplaced angst.

The Sabbath was a technology that embraced the futility of how you got here and what happened to you once you left. That's why you kissed the ass of a goat and called it the devil's face. It was a ritual so liberating, so debasing; it made it impossible to take yourself seriously. All you could do was let go, relax, and renounce your faith in anything except the feeling of being alive and amusing yourself by the random prophetic gestures of a goat everyone decided was the devil for the evening. In this account from southern France, you can see the medicine of the scapegoat still working in the psyche. It disarms the practitioner of all pressures in the world. All guilt and all shame evaporate instantly on the Sabbath.

They said that the place of meeting was commonly a fountain in the wood of Mosslaines, about a league distant from Arras, and that they sometimes went thither on foot. The more usual way of proceeding, however, according to their own account, was this— they took an ointment given to them by the devil, with which they anointed a wooden rod, at the fame time rubbing the palms of their hands with it, and then, placing the rod between their legs, they were suddenly carried through the air to the place of assembly. They found there a multitude of people, of both sexes, and of all estates and ranks, even wealthy burghers and nobles—and one of the persons examined declared that he had feen there not only ordinary ecclesiastics, but bishops and even cardinals. They found tables already spread, covered with all forts of meats, and abundance of wines. A devil presided, usually in the form of a goat, with the tail of an ape, and a human countenance. Each first did oblation and homage to him by offering him his or her foul, or, at least fome part of their body, and then, as a mark of adoration, kissed him on the posteriors.

Sadly, etiquette's pen treats these rituals harshly in our history books. The same religion that invented the scapegoat would end up burning anyone who practiced its adoration. It makes you wonder if etiquette would have approved if the goat had been tossed off a cliff instead of kissed.

The Sabbath included the need-fire, the ancient priapic rite. Zoroaster believed that which survives in fire is pure; everything else is facade. Fire exposes facade. The flame is a window into a chapel. Like the giants, fire loses its purity when propagated and is best made fresh from human calories. Pure fire exists dormant in all things. You must need the fire to appear before it can awake. All fires must be extinguished to make a virgin birth.

The eve of St. John was one of the most important days of the medieval year. The need-fire—or the St. John's fire, was kindled just at midnight, the moment when the solstice was supposed to take place, and the young people of both sexes danced round it, and, above all things, leaped over it, or rushed through it, which was looked upon not only as a purification, but as a protection against evil influences. It was the night when ghosts and other beings of the spiritual world were abroad, and when witches had most power.

The limping of Priapus is best seen in the symbology of Saint Peter, who was crucified upside down. Peter is a symbol of the phallus, hence the inverted cross. An entire new church was built on the inversion of Priapus, and no one batted an eye. This shouldn't be hard to believe, considering this was the same time we started calling it 1 AD. Man wanted to step away from his past and move on. And so he did. All it took was a scorched city, a desire to change, and lots and lots of syphilis.

Recently, St. Mary of the Ovaries changed its name to Southwark Cathedral. It's founding as a nunnery turned out to be more of a sequestered brothel next to the ferry house crossing the Thames. Once exposed, the shame was too much to bear, and the six hundred-year-old church erased its history.

The Hebrew mind saw the past as being ahead of you. You see it clearly because it has already happened. The future, however, was still at your back. It hasn't been brought into view yet. In ancient times, the axis of thinking was flipped. The east was the time of the ancients. A Phoenician sentence emerged from its dawn on the page and traveled its way west. Egyptian hieroglyphs were ambidextrous. In the sixth century BC, the Greeks added vowels and swapped the direction from left to right. Hebrew was always written as action to noun instead of noun to action. Everything inverted when consciousness rose up from the ecliptic.

On April 15th 2019 two things happened. The sun crossed the analemma and the ceiling of Notre Dame's cathedral burned to the ground. Three years later, on the day of the anniversary of the fire, on the spot where the spire landed on the Cathedral floor, a lead sarcophagus was uncovered dated to the 14th Century. This is the story of Osiris. The gargoyles were giggling with mischief from the roof over this one

. Apparently, the cathedral needed some fresh air, and the Saints were airlifted in a rapture by helicopter in the middle of the day. In 2017, the Vatican issued rules about the treatment of relics. It requires their movement to be done in discretion out of the eyes of the public. Instead, the statues of sixteen Saints were decapitated on live tv with oxyacetylene. The rooster at the top of the spire that burned carried a piece from the crown of thorns. This symbol of Christ fell into the fire in a bonfire of the Phoenix. St Thomas is the only Saint on the roof who was looking up at the Rooster Christ. Thomas always knew this would happen. It's the main reason his book was side-lined to the apocrypha. The Rooster Christ had been Priapus this whole time mounted on top of the Virgin Mary. The horned Venus strikes again.

The internet will one day turn the collective unconscious into the collective conscious. There will continue to be growing pains along the way. We can reclaim rejected plasma by embracing the dowsing rods of ecstasy and epiphany. This is why we find God when the almond meets the phallus. Priapus is a posture. It's the primal erection of curiosity, not seriousness.

CHAPTER TEN

The Baptism

Having the idea to circumcise a child shouldn't be normal. The fact we're still doing this in the age of victimhood tells you how important this ritual must be for the spirit. Perhaps carving away at our genitals is the only way to revisit a core wound. Having so many taboos around sex shouldn't be normal, either. Movies show blood, gore, violence, mayhem, murder, abuse, and psychopathy, but not sex. That's where the movie draws its line. All of these things show us the shadows of a primal wound.

Three days and nights they inflict punishment bodily in hell, and then he beholds bodily those three days' happiness in heaven. - Knowledge from the Zand 30:13

A survivor of trauma will employ self-blame to heal. It seeks a reason for the trauma to return to a world of justice. Self-mutilation is a technology victims use to manage care. The unseen wound must be revealed. The denial bleeds a cut to the surface. Cutters find relief through the ritual cutting of skin because the blood is proof of a wound. The wound secretes a chemical high but so does exercise. This isn't about the high; it's about the primal wound. We find satisfaction in hurting ourselves. The self-mutilation of biting your nails is therapeutic. The better we understand this technology, the better we see its energy.

John wore clothes made of camel's hair. He had a leather strap around his waist and ate grasshoppers and wild honey. - Matthew 3:4

Forty-four verses in the Bible reference wearing camel hair or sackcloth, and six verses on covering oneself in ashes. The Old Testament is a story of millions of people who needed something innocent to die to pay for their wickedness. That mindset forged a path to self-mutilation. The fact that we keep coming up with excuses to mutilate our genitals under the auspice of sanitation proves we're nursing a core wound. The literal Hebrew definition of the word covenant is "the coveted slice of meat." The first cleavage was a covenant of the zygote. It is both preservation and sacrifice in a single act.

In my flesh I complete what is lacking in Christ's afflictions, for the sake of his body, that is the Church. - Colossians 1:24

Afghan Shiite Muslims observe Ashura with public demonstrations of bloody self-mutilation in commemoration of the day Noah left the Ark. The body remembers when it was cleaved. These rituals have been happening for thousands of years. The desire to self-harm is instinctive, and ritual is our excuse to get the blood rolling. Pain is part of their ceremony because the pain was medicine.

And they cried aloud and cut themselves after their custom with swords and lances, until the blood gushed out upon them. - 1 Kings 18:28

* * *

Circumcision was a trauma monopoly for Jews and Christians. These were ritual blood cults that went mainstream.

Every male among you shall be circumcised ... it will be the sign of the covenant between me and you. - Genesis 17:10-11

The desire to mutilate was stronger even when Leviticus told them not to.

"Do not cut your bodies for the dead or put tattoo marks on yourselves." - Leviticus 19:28

Make up your mind Bible. Should I cut myself or not?

No foreigner uncircumcised in heart and flesh is to enter my sanctuary. - Ezekiel 44:7–9

The Saints were elite masochists who self-mutilated by proxy. We call them martyrs, but when you review what happened to each of them, you realize they were people who willingly sought out mutilation and were raised on a pedestal in proportion to how much it hurt. No one was making them do this. Nor was anyone making the congregation do this. This was early man learning how to regulate his psyche.

The Saints of Masochism
  Saint Andrew was tied to a tree and scourged.
  Saint Agnes was brotheled, burned, throat sworded.
  Saint Bartholomew was skinned alive, then beheaded.
  Saint Catherine broke on a wheel.
  Saint Clement tied to an anchor and cast into sea.
  Saint Dymphna was beheaded by father.

Saint Eulalia was tortured in 13 ways.
Saint Hippolytus was torn apart by wild horses.
Saint Ignatius was eaten by lions.
Saint James was stoned and clubbed.
Saint Jerome was flailed.
Saint John was scalped and eaten alive.
Saint Lawrence was roasted alive.
Saint Matthias was burned alive.
Saint Matthew was stabbed.
Saint Paul was beheaded.
Saint Peter was crucified upside down, cut in half.
Saint Philip was crucified.
Saint Phocas was thrown in a kiln and boiled alive.
Saint Symphorosa saw children murdered, drowned.
Saint Thomas was martyred by four spears.
Saint Victor was ground dead in a stone mill.

Jesus said he came to Jerusalem to be crucified. His goal was to become the ultimate scapegoat and martyr. People were cleansing their sins through animal sacrifice. Jesus wanted to end the Passover sacrifice by being the last. He was the ultimate animal rights activist. Circumcision was always a kind of animal sacrifice. The same circuit is employed as a way for man to dump energy, manifested as forgiveness. Man is forgiven of his electricity in his sacrifice. We are learning to work the circuit.

Martyr originally meant witness or testimony. It originally applied to Apostles, but it became so popular it was generalized to those who suffered hardships for their faith. Eventually, it was restricted to those who had died. Martyrdom requires two ingredients — suffering and witness. The Pharisees and Sadducees would have capitalized on martyr technology the same way they did animal sacrifice technology. In 1782, Godfrey Higgins compiled a list of messiah-like saviors who were crucified in exchange for ascension. Notice how the frequency of saviors increases in the approach to 1 AD. This timeline shows early man crawling out of obedience and into mercy, the two pillars of the shepherd's crook.

Higgins' Messiahs
Thulis of Egypt in 1700 BC
Krishna of India in 1200 BC
Crite of Chaldea in 1200 BC
Atys of Phrygia in 1170 BC
Tammuz of Syria in 1160 BC
Hesus of Eros in 834 BC
Bali of Orissa in 725 BC
Indra of Tibet in 725 BC
Iao of Nepal in 622 BC
Buddha Sakia in 600 BC
Mithra in 600 BC
Alcestos in 600 BC
Quezalcoatl in 587 BC
Wittoba in 552 BC
Prometheus in 547 BC
Quirinus of Rome in 506 BC.

There was a man sent from God whose name was John. He came as a witness to testify concerning that light, so that through him all might believe. He himself was not the light; he came only as a witness to the light. - John 1:6-8

Is it any surprise the same guy who ate bugs in a hairshirt was a masochist, too? John the Baptist had become addicted to the near-death experience. In the Jordan river, he had perfected the art of drowning with help from his friends. Waterboarding is simulated drowning. So too, is baptism if done correctly. But John wasn't doing this for any ceremony of forgiveness. John wanted to see God's face.

It was morning. John was angry when his friends pulled him out of the water too early again. He had assured them they were absolved of any sin should he die. John was approaching the gates and getting closer every time. It took several men to hold John underwater long enough to be reborn. But it worked. He emerged a sobbing baby with fresh eyes. Everyone saw how much he glowed. How different he was rising out of the water. Every face he greeted was painted with the glory from his cheeks. His hands were as soft as feathers. Every breath seemed to be made of gold. His smile put tears in everyone's eyes. God had revealed his face and John saw it. Someone called out as if congratulating him, "The Living Water!"

People asked John to baptize them next. They saw his technology and knew it was better than what they had. Don't mistake today's baptism ceremony for the ceremonies of the times in the Bible. These rituals were playing for keeps. In the Tabernacle, family pets were deeply loved and nurtured for years, only to have their arteries' emptied in a pit for a few moments of psychological comfort. If losing their family pet wasn't enough, they could mutilate themselves in the name of repentance. When that wasn't enough, they would kill anyone around them who disagreed. It doesn't matter how; all wounds must come to the surface, even if the wound is in someone else's chest.

Saul replied, "Say to David, 'The king wants no other price for the bride than a hundred Philistine foreskins, to take revenge on his enemies.'" Saul's plan was to have David fall by the hands of the Philistines. - 1 Samuel 18:25

If you grasp man's mind at the time of Christ, it becomes easy to believe and understand his story. Christ had technology like no other. He was the living alchemist living in the land of sacrifice. He saw what was foretold in the stars, his coming into Rome and undergoing a Sundance ritual. He would create the ultimate uber-martyr that would end all martyrs.

From that time on Jesus began to explain to his disciples that he must go to Jerusalem and suffer many things at the hands of the elders, the chief priests and the teachers of the law, and that he must be killed and on the third day be raised to life. - Matthew 16:21

The Arma Christi are the weapons of Christ and the instruments of the Passion. There are twenty-six instruments of pain in total, and each of them allows one to meditate on the torture and passion of Christ.

Cross of Christ, Crown of Thorn, Pillar of Flagellation, Sponge, Lance, Nails, Veil of Veronica, Sceptre Reed, Purple Robe, Titulus Crucis, Grail, Robe, Dice, Rooster, Vessel of Gall and Vinegar, Ladder, Hammer, Pincers, Vessel of Myrrh, Shroud, Eclipse, Thirty Silver, Spitting Face, Hand, Chains, Lantern, Sword, Judas, Trumpet

These instruments were arms of heraldry and pride. This technology satisfied an ancient hunger. At their heart, all wounds are hunger. If mankind came from a place of shame from a deeply suppressed wound in our past, we would expect to see a heavy salvation technology at work in our culture. We'd see a fetish for slavery and tools like scapegoating, mutilation, virtue-signaling, martyrdom, self-flagellation, crusadism, and denialism at work in everything we do. And we do. We see every one of those things right now. We have seen them at work for a long time.

The Church, the State, and the Alchemist benefited from

the Crucifixion. All three participated in the ritual voluntarily. Jesus came to the garden. The State placed him on a cross. The Church witnessed his sacrifice and wrote it down. Rome formalized religion and gave it its first bureaucracy. Cicero coined religio as a bureaucratic concept for "the proper performance of rites in veneration of the gods." Rome was the first to mine that sweet spot between faith and bureaucracy. These vectors are the Church's true cross.

Rome did not write the Bible. They compiled it. Rome had little choice in the stories that would make it onto the page. Mythology is the unwavering appetite of the ancients. The politicians of Rome were not leading the people. They were following them. They attached themselves to the mouth of its leviathan. Rome wrote nothing. They dictated what the mythology had already been saying. Rome did what it did best. It swallowed a culture by embracing it. They anthropomorphized the sky clock, helped Abraxas from the sea, and connected his circuit to the heavens.

CHAPTER ELEVEN
Garden of Eden

In the beginning God created the heavens and the earth. - Genesis 1:1

The very first word of the Bible is transliterated as bereshiyt, a word that means in the summit of something. It's normal for linguists to translate this as "In the beginning"; however it is more accurate to say "In beginning" as there's nothing to suggest this is a singular event. But there's more. The text really said, "In the summit of God created the everything." This is a different sentence from "In the beginning God created the heaven and the earth."

The zygote represents the first stage in the development of a genetically unique organism. The zygote is endowed with genes from two parents, and thus it is diploid (carrying two sets of chromosomes). The joining of haploid gametes to produce a diploid zygote is a common feature in the sexual reproduction of all organisms except bacteria. - Wikipedia 1:2

God is a union of phallus and vulva. Genesis 1:1 talks about the union of man and woman in orgasm, the summit of God. The Garden of Eden is a play-by-play of your less-than-immaculate conception and the experience of your one-cell-old zygote, the fertilized ovum. Its memory, and experience, are reflected in the collective unconscious through the Garden of Eden. Genesis was your first cleave, the very first time you split your zygote. And you've been twinning yourself ever since. Over and over again.

Cleavage, in embryology, is the first few cellular divisions of a zygote (fertilized egg). Initially, the zygote splits along a longitudinal plane. The second division is also longitudinal, but at 90 degrees to the plane of the first. The third division is perpendicular to the first two and is equatorial in position. - Google Answers 3:4

Your zygote separates the waters from the waters making the heavens and the earth. This is the process of longitudinal cleavage. In Genesis 1:2, the zygote has cleaved, but its organism lacks organs. Its face is dark because its body has no form.

The earth was without form and void, and darkness was over the face of the deep. And the Spirit of God was hovering over the face of the waters. - Genesis 1:2

In today's world, the Son of Man is a ten-day-old artificially supported blastocyst living in a test tube in a lab. The tube is a virgin womb artificially inseminated by a creator. It sounds like an awful way to grow up, but this is what man calls progress sometimes. Think of all the work and marketing that went into remote-operated robot surgery when you can't help but wonder why they don't just buy a plane ticket. But the healthcare industry is a predator in scrubs controlled by a government that says there's too many people, so it's easy to see how these kinds of things will happen. This is a jungle, and the only people hiding are prey. So the human blastocyst enters the service industry as an indentured servant born inside the confines of a corporate Eden. All from the world where child labor and slavery were proudly prohibited.

No one has noticed that none of this progress has unlocked any door or found any key. The egg will always require the prerequisite of chicken, and the chicken will always require the egg. The DNA was here at genesis. Sure we can hack chickens. We can copy them and warm them to open in incubators. But the network came with the code of chicken already installed. Every new chick instantiates itself from a precompiled library to prevent memory leaks. Programmers call these leaks memory holes. It's a place in the code where a created object is never reaped or cleaned. This can wreak havoc on a system that is trying to run forever. As seconds pile on the clock, the garbage is never emptied, bringing an entire universe to its knees. This is why the mafia likes the garbage business. It shorts the entire circuit. Death works the same way. We are born in a mortal network that requires our death to play. It's the only way a massive online multi-player consciousness could exist. Everything must be created and destroyed at genesis. Every mortal is born with death. This is why neither the chicken nor the egg came first — they were spawned.

After he drove the man out, he placed on the east side of the Garden of Eden cherubim and a flaming sword flashing back and forth to guard the way to the tree of life. - Genesis 3:24

Every day new life dawns in the east. East is the doorway to Eden. The egg is claimed once the cherubim take their post. Cherubim is a group of cherubs with the head of an ox, lion, eagle, and man, a genetic ark. The sperm posts them at the entrance of the egg, so other sperm know God is already there.

The Garden is filled with passionate fruit. The biting of the apple is ejaculation. The flaming sword is the zinc flash seen when an egg is fertilized. The flash is the "banishment" of Adam and Eve into mortality. The zygote experiences this separation into boy or girl. He cleaves himself in two and begins a lifelong process of dividing himself again and again.

A river watering the garden flowed from Eden; from there it was separated into four headwaters. - Genesis 2:10

The ovary has four headwaters. In the myometrium, the uterine artery branches four times. In Aramaic, Eden means fruitful, like an ovary. Eden is home to the Tree of Life and the Tree of Knowledge. An artery is a tree of life and a vein is a tree of knowledge. The Garden is the ovary. Inside the walls of its epithelium, you see the roots of a sacred tree in a grove of vine-bearing ova. The fruit of the ovary is so satisfying it could only be forbidden. You could not compress a reproductive anatomy lesson any better than the story of the Garden of Eden. The accuracy of the syncretism between biology and mythology is striking. It's as if we knew the science of the fertility process thousands of years ago, long before we even got here. All mythology is epigenetic wisdom.

CHAPTER TWELVE

Another Side of Adam

A protoplast is the first creator. It comes from oneself. Adam and Eve were the same person separated. The Talmud explains that Adam is the spirit and Eve is the soul. This is how our tetradic body is cleaved. All of us live with the ghost of a missing person. None of us have been reunited with this other half. All we can do is share the feeling of something missing. This is the longing behind love. This is much of the yearning behind feeling alone. These are ancient wounds that foster intimacy. We will always be searching for our missing copilot.

And God had divided (paradise) between us, between me and your mother Eve, so that we might guard it. As for me, he had given me the eastern and northern portion; to your mother Eve he had entrusted the southern and the western portion. - The Book of Adam - 7:3

In the Book of Adam, when Eve died, she made her final prayer.

"Lord, do not alienate me from Adam's place, but command me, me

also, (to be) with him, as we both were in paradise, inseparable from one another. Do not separate us in our death, but place me where you have placed him." And after this prayer she gave up her soul. - Book of Adam, 42:5-8

The Vitruvian Adam was before the cleaving of his seed. One could call the Vitruvian a hermaphrodite or an androgyne. The Elohim were Vitruvian. And whether we think of them as hermaphrodites or androgyne the essence is the same.

In 1945, the Apocalypse of Adam appeared at Nag Hammadi in upper Egypt. It is a Sethian work from the second century. In it, a 700-year-old Adam tells his son Seth that God chose to divide him and Eve into male and female, making them mortal. When the Hindu deity Shiva unites with his consort Shakti he becomes Ardhanarishvara, whose name means the lord who is half a woman. Ardhanari means half male and half female, or the androgyne. There are many reasons to consider the androgyne of Adam and Eve. Two contrary stories in Genesis about the exact origins of man have led to one of the longest debates in the history of theology. In essence, this debate boils down to two interpretations. In Genesis 1, Adam and Eve are created simultaneously.

So God created mankind in his own image, in the image of God he created them; male and female he created them. - Genesis 1:27

In Genesis 2, Adam is divided into two.

So the Lord God caused the man to fall into a deep sleep; and while he was sleeping, he took one of the man's ribs and then closed up the place with flesh. - Genesis 2:21

A verse in Psalms translated back into the original Hebrew

suggests the idea of a two-faced Adam, made from the beginning.

You have formed me before and behind - Psalms 139:5

When you translate rib back into Hebrew, you realize it can mean the entire side of the body.

"'He took one of his ribs' means an entire side of his body because the word "tzel'a" is used in the book of Exodus to refer to one side of the holy Tabernacle. A similar discussion can be found in Leviticus Rabbah 14:1 where R. Levi states: "When man was created, he was created with two body-fronts, and He [God] sawed him in two, so that two backs resulted, one back for the male and another for the female." - Mark Sameth

This is why the word Adam is not used in Hebrew as a proper name the first five times it appears in the text. It is not until Genesis 4:1, when Adam becomes mortal and copulates with Eve, that he is considered an actual human.

Adam made love to his wife Eve, and she became pregnant and gave birth to Cain. She said, "With the help of the Lord I have brought forth a man." - Genesis 4:1

The ash ligature holds the truth of Adam and Eve. The first man was Ædam, the hermaphrodite. Ædam was spilt into two. Their names became Adam and Eve. The Old English ligature was named after the Ash Tree rune, Ansuz. This rune is a single trunk split into twin branches.

Why do we feel shame when we are naked? If shame came from the exposure of genitals, one would feel shame from the lips. This doesn't happen because shame is specific to the pudendum, where the sexual organs reside. The source of man's shame comes from a place where he feels something missing. Inadequacy is a flavor of nakedness. We know something's missing because our zygote was conscious at conception. The biting of the apple meant the loss of androgyny.

Adam and his wife were both naked, and they felt no shame. - Genesis 2:25

Shame is felt for the first time after Adam splits in two. His shame originates from the part that is missing. The shame you feel when naked is proof. The place where you feel it is its origin. The Egyptians would call this shame your ka. It is the energy of something that is no longer there. Phantom limb syndrome is a condition where a person has an itch on the part of the body that's no longer attached. The conscious body still holds its original shape, and everything lost will naturally radiate an imprint of what used to be there. That imprint is how shame feels.

This is why it feels so good to find someone with the parts we are missing. We call this feeling being in love because we feel at home. This surrogate homecoming feels so good we crave more intimacy. We don't feel shame when naked with a lover because the piece we miss is finally home. We long to join these missing twins forever in a binding ritual where we join them together somehow, and so we do by smooshing our genitals as close to each other as we can. We get so excited about this because every part of our body feels this is how it was always supposed to be, and we orgasm. In unison. Hopefully. When we don't, we realize these missing genitals that feel so good aren't our own. They sure do feel like them, though. We thought they were and wanted to try them on. This is why half of all marriages don't end in divorce; they end in realization.

* * *

The man said, "This is now bone of my bones and flesh of my flesh; she shall be called 'woman,' for she was taken out of man." - Genesis 2:23

The original text refers to Eve as "he." The Hebrew text translates as "he will be called out woman." The devout translator will correct this anomaly and pat himself on the back. Meanwhile, the truth is corrupted. This happens little by little every few years.

And the girl was very beautiful and attractive, chaste and modest, and unmarried. And she went down to the well, filled her water jar, and came up. - Genesis 24:16

In Genesis 24:16, the original Hebrew refers to Rebekah at the beginning of the verse as a young boy, not a young girl. In Genesis 12:8, Abram's tent is "her tent."

Genesis 12:8 - From there he went on toward the hills east of Bethel and pitched [her] tent, with Bethel on the west and Ai on the east.

There are eleven misgendered tent anomalies in Genesis. More than any other book in the Bible. There are twenty in total throughout the entire Old Testament. There is one anomaly like this in the Book of Psalms. The gender blur seems to disappear as the generations of Adam beget children. These gender anomalies appear most often in the Book of Ezekiel. Islam refers to the prophet Ezekiel as Dhu al-Kifl or the one who possesses the double.

The gender-switching cases are not mistakes or scribal errors. They are examples of what the second century Jerusalem scribe Ben Sira called the "twists," "obscurities," "riddles," and "hidden things" of the Torah. Whatever the intentions of the biblical writers may or may not have been, as the contemporary Bible scholar James L. Kugel has observed, "the first assumption that all ancient interpreters seem to share is that the Bible is a fundamentally cryptic document." - Mark Sameth

Guillaume Postel (16th century) and Michelangelo Lanci (19th century) knew the God of Israel was understood by the ancient priests to be a singular, dual-gendered deity. They paid dearly for talking about it. Postel barely survived the Inquisition and was imprisoned by the church, while Lanci was shown mercy by being stripped of all his commissions.

YHWH in Hebrew spells He-She when you open its name like a Torah Ark. This Ark is a two-door cabinet used to preserve the word of God. YH is on the left door. WH is on the right. Once opened, these letters reveal the dual-gendered name of God. Elijah is made from Eli, Hu, and Yah, which means "My God He is She." Elohim is El (male) - O (female) - Im (plural), also know as "that." According to the Zohar, the purpose of Deuteronomy 6:4 is so the male and female would join as one.

Hear, O Israel: The Lord our God, the Lord is one. - Deuteronomy 6:4

The Zohar has a lot of commentary on the dual-gendered name of god and the Vitruvian Adam.

When souls issue from heaven, they issue male and female, as one; it is only as they descend that they separate. - The Zohar

Atum, the original Adam, was called the "The Complete One." He was a primordial self-creating hermaphroditic god that rose from the waters. Atum came from Heliopolis, the city of the stone phallus, or obelisk. Amun from Thebes would absorb Atum and hide his identity as a hermaphroditic god behind the veil of the sphinx — the divine chimera.

The Rebis in alchemy is considered the final result of The Great Work. This is the divine hermaphrodite and is symbolized as a double-headed male/female figure filtered and separated by the energies of the Sun and Moon. Rebis is the Red Queen and White King combined. The Rebis of man and Shekhinah is an essential theme in the Zohar, "Just as She is called by the name of the male, so He too is called by Her name." Ecstacy is the union of what's missing.

According to Gnostic thought, Adam Kasia is the first Adam, the hidden Adam. Hawa Kasia is the hidden Eve. Our eyes never see them. We see only see Adam Patria, the bodily Adam. Jewish tradition calls this Adam Kadmon. The idea of a primordial Adam is important because this is our original form made in the image of the Elohim.

They are Right and Left, they are spirit and soul; they are called Adam and Eve. - The Secret Adam

A chromosome is a chromo soma, a color body. Every cell in the human body has twin color bodies inside except for two. The egg and the sperm have no twin. They are missing their side, or as the Bible calls it, they are missing a rib. Fertilization is when these two amputees find each other. Like the cell, you are a much larger human color body. You are also missing a side. The chimeric channel inside you is your missing twin's seat. This is the primal androgyne and hermaphrodite. Your Ka is more than your body. Your Ka is you before you were amputated.

"Out of them, the one who had the male form became known as the

Manu named Svāyambhuva, and the woman became known as Śatarūpā, the queen of the great soul Manu." - Bhagavata Purana 3.12.52

This dichotomy of male or female originates at meiosis, when a cell divides to produce gametes or sex cells missing half of their light bodies (chromosomes).

The way Genesis 2:23 is worded suggests this is Adam's second attempt at getting a woman. The scripture reads, "This one finally is bone from my bones." This idea of a beta version of Eve gave birth to the rise of Lilith, the first Eve. Her name is referenced only once in Isaiah as a night demon.

Wildcats will meet hyenas, the goat demon will call to his friends, and there Lilith will lurk and find her resting place. - Isaiah 34:14

The Talmud speculates quite seriously she complained too much, so Adam sent her back to the factory. One story says she bled too much, and it repulsed Adam. But if we think like an Egyptian, we can see Lilith is Eve's ka. In Genesis 2:24, Adam is told he should cleave unto Eve.

Therefore shall a man leave his father and his mother, and shall cleave unto his wife: and they shall be one flesh. - Genesis 2:23-24

Ka is the spirit of one's entire entity, missing parts and all. Lilith is the shadow cleaved from the making of Eve. When Ædam becomes man, he is cleaved of his Eve. This missing spirit of the night is the Lilith. This is why Lilith is associated with imposter syndrome. She is a phantom who can never be found physically. According to tradition, Lilith seduces husbands, bares them children, and becomes so enraged she kills them all. She has a male counterpart who does the same.

Lillith's demon is given dominion over children until their

circumcision. Nine days for boys. Twenty for girls. Lilith has dominion because their ka remains attached to their sacred wound. The ritual of circumcision is popular because it tries to overwrite the loss with another loss that's smaller. But this doesn't work. Lilith's demon murders her new family because it doesn't heal her core wound. All it did was show Lilith a side of her was still missing.

CHAPTER THIRTEEN

Hermaphroditus

Aphrodite, the goddess of love and beauty, was wooed by Hermes. She had rejected him, so Hermes sought the help of Zeus. Zeus sent an eagle to take away Aphrodite's sandal when she was bathing and gave it to Hermes. When Aphrodite came looking for the sandal, Hermes made love to her. She bore him a son, Hermaphroditus, portrayed in Greco-Roman art as a female figure with male genitals. According to Apollo, Hermes was kind of a dick. But did you know he also had a vulva? Hermes not only fathered Hermaphroditus; he was one himself. Note his symbol is the female symbol with horns. Hermes is the Horned Aphrodite. Or, if you prefer Greek, Mercury is the Horned Venus.

Ovid has a famous story of Hermaphroditus, but it seems to be a recycled story of his mother with the roles reversed. Ovid paints Hermaphroditus and hermaphroditism as a cursed affliction resulting from a supernatural rape in a stream that turns men into hermaphrodites who enter its waters. But in the ancient Greek city of Halicarnassus, the story of the hermaphrodite is different. A poem found on one of its walls near the Spring of Salmacis reads in Greek:

* * *

Halicarnassus settles the lovely hill beside the stream of Salmacis, called dear to the immortals in song, and she occupies the lovely home of the nymph, who once took our boy in her sweet embrace and raised him, Hermaphroditus, to be outstanding, he who discovered marriage and was the first to bind the marriage bed in law. And she herself [Salmacis] beneath the holy streams dripping in the cave tames the savage mind of men.

Lucian of Samosata would also correct Ovid by saying the boy's condition was inherited from Hermes. The idea of a stream that "tames the savage mind of men" is reminiscent of the production of estrogen in the true hermaphrodite. The invention of marriage being attributed to Hermaphroditus makes perfect sense if you consider the union of marriage based on the union of the hermaphrodite's genitals and fits the mythology perfectly. Ovid is doing what any historian would do. He was protecting the reader from things they could not understand. It didn't fit Ovid's idea of who Hermes should be. Ovid chooses to make the nymph his scapegoat and cleanse his story for mass consumption, causing Hermaphroditus to suffer the same fate as Priapus.

It would be accurate to assume most of the Patriarchs and early progenitor gods were Nephilim-like Hermaphrodites. The divine twin protoplast race existed in every culture. All of the Titans were hermaphroditic, or double twins, who stimulated the early population. The only reason mythology doesn't push this more is because it's uncomfortable to accept. We don't want it in our mythology, and Ovid is here to help.

"We rise in the presence of the Supernal King and male unites with female." - The Zohar

Statues of Hermes, called herms, were common in the ancient world and symbols of fertility. They were intended to bring prosperity and luck. A herm might be found outside any house. They were square pillars equipped with male genitals; on top of each was the head of Hermes. They marked areas as sacred or designated the bounds of one's home.

According to Plato, Aphrodite was born without a mother from the spilled foam of Uranus' severed genitals after Cronus cast them out into the sea. Like Ezekiel, Aphrodite is a double deity known as the Lady of Cythera and the Lady of Cypris. The male Aphroditus was the same image as Aphrodite but with a phallus.

"There's also a statue of Venus on Cyprus, that's bearded, shaped and dressed like a woman, with scepter and male genitals, and they conceive her as both male and female. Aristophanes calls her Aphroditus, and Laevius says: Worshiping, then, the nurturing god Venus, whether she is male or female, just as the Moon is a nurturing goddess. In his Atthis Philochorus, too, states that she is the Moon and that men sacrifice to her in women's dress, women in men's, because she is held to be both male and female." - Macrobius

According to genes, there are three sexes, not two. This is not a slippery slope. It's what you see under a microscope. A natural process exists whereby two fertilized eggs or young embryos of opposite sexes fuse to develop into a single baby. This is the true hermaphrodite. Hermaphroditic goats aren't an oddity. When two naturally hornless goats breed, one in five offspring is a hermaphrodite.

There are outcrossers, and there are selfers in the plant world. Selfers have both the anther and the ovule, while the outcrossers are missing one and require the services of bees. This is why the birds and the bees are a euphemism for sex. Hermaphroditic vegetation needs no sex to reproduce because it was not split into an Adam and an Eve. If we were plants, the primordial Ædam is monoecious, and the cleaved

Adam and Eve were dioecious.

Even today, more species in the world do express hermaphroditism than do not express it. The mangrove killifish, rivulus marmoratus, has both sex organs and still reproduces this way in a process called selfing. As every creature is unpacked from the ark and spawned on earth's terrain, their reproductive needs morph to fill the tank.

CHAPTER FOURTEEN

Lamassupians

Taylor Muhl is her own twin. She carries two sets of DNA. She has two immune systems, and she passes cells between two bloodstreams. Taylor's chimerism is visible down the middle of her body. You can see a difference in skin pigmentation from her left side to her right. You see chimerism in animals where one half, or one eye, is a different color. This isn't a genetic defect, a disease, or a handicap. Chimerism is when a body expresses two or more distinct genes, and it is noticeable. A hermaphrodite is a specific type of chimera.

In 1995, Anton Krzyzanowski was born a girl. There was no DNA test. By the time Anton was 13, he was in full-blown male puberty. Anton has ovotestis, a gonad with both testicular and ovarian aspects. Glandula hermaphroditica is a standard anatomical feature in the reproductive system of many organisms. Anton is one of them.

Anton's family committed him to a monastery believing that "demons were inside him," and he was advised to pray to become a normal woman. Upon closer inspection, the hospital confirmed Anton had no uterus. Anton faced a lot of abuse for expressing his chimerism.

In Thebes, Amun was called the hidden one. He replaced Atum, the sacred hermaphrodite from Heliopolis. Amun often was portrayed as a sphinx. Even the hermaphroditic gods were forced into hiding.

The frequency of polydactyly, hermaphroditism, and twinning declined with the giants. These features were no longer necessary to spawn a race. It's easy to see how chimerism affected politics and religion. The idea of royalty associated with a chimeric being, such as the Pegasus or the winged lion, harkens back to a time when chimerism was not shunned but worshipped as a ruling class.

Every human body is built on a chimeric platform. Each of us has a sidecar for genetic passengers. There is no way of counting how many of us display chimerism because it can happen from organ to organ. There are cases where a mother's DNA fails to identify her as the parent of a child because her uterus has different DNA. Even organ transplant is a kind of chimerism. In vitro fertilization seems even to encourage it.

Tetragametic chimerism is formed from the merging of two nonidentical twins. Natural chimeras are formed from at least four parent cells, each with a unique population sharing a single host. As chimeras, we can be four things at once. This is the meaning of the Eagle, the Lion, the Ox, and the Man. The Sumerians called this creature the Lamassu. It is the sphinx, the four-headed face of God. The Assyrians decorated their doorways and gates with them. These winged bull-men represented the zodiac and set a room's bearings to the sky clock's cross.

The Lamassu are always in pairs. They are twin preservers. Their name translates to "protective spirits." The Lamassu were guardians of the gates. Like Noah, they were a preserver. Nimrud is considered a possible site for the Tower of Babel. Here we see the chimeras of Lamassu associated with deluge preservation. They were depicted with five legs. This feature is only noticeable from their sides as you pass through their portal. Outside its portal, the Lamassu are stationary. Inside, however, they are dynamic and moving. This embodies the transformative symbology of a gate. The Lamassu is mentioned in the Epic of Gilgamesh because they represent a promise to preserve mankind in his movement between two worlds.

CHAPTER FIFTEEN

Mystery of the Sphinx

A lazy mind will comprehend truth once and stop. It sees no reason to go deeper. But pirates bury treasure under treasure all the time. They are clever. There are four gospels in the Roman sky clock. Mathew is the symbol of man, the Aquarius. Mark is the symbol of Leo, the lion. Luke is the bull of Taurus. And John is the eagle of Scorpio. The four gospels are the divine chimera of the zodiac.

Each of the four had the face of a human being, and on the right side each had the face of a lion, and on the left the face of an ox; each also had the face of an eagle. - Ezekiel 1:10

Regulus, or Alpha Leonis, is the brightest object in the constellation Leo and one of the brightest stars in the night sky. Regulus is "the heart of the lion" in the chest of the constellation. Latin for prince or little king, Babylonians called it Sharru, "star of the Lion's breast." The wandering stars are on a never-ending quest to Regulus, the home of their newborn king. Every year they make a pilgrimage through the Lion's Gate. The retrograde orbits of each make a heavenly drama unfold as they seem to bow and curtsey before their king.

All eyes were on the Sphinx above and below. Underneath the Sphinx is a reported hidden chamber or library. This is the Ark of the Sphinx. It seems impossible for this not to be true, considering the stele (stone tablet) found on the chest of the Sphinx listing the name of Egypt's king. The Sphinx was the sarcophagus of Egypt, its living egg, and the King's stele was the cartouche binding it to the land. The first deluge was the story of Osiris traveling through the underworld's waters, the original flood. He was guided by a chimera through the portal into everlasting life or resurrection.

The divine chimera is encrypted in Jewish exegesis as the four aspects of understanding source. The first is the bull (p'shat), who takes source literally and considers his understanding whole. He will call things objective and insist there is a singular perspective. The man (Remez) is wiser than the bull. He sees the hint in something and can form a perspective depending on what he's looking for. The lion (Drash) is wiser than man. He considers the lessons of source and its oracle as a creative force. Finally, there is the eagle (Sod). His source is archetypal. The eagle decrypts all secrets. These four are called the Orchard in the Talmud. They reference the Garden of Eden because the Vitruvian Man is all four combined.

Four rabbis enter the orchard. One looked and died; one looked and went mad; One looked and apostatized; One entered in peace and departed in peace. - The Zohar

The divine chimera is a living orchard inside you. You sense reality through each of its pores: Matthew the man, Mark the lion, Luke the ox, and John the eagle. This is why tetramorph is so prevalent in our mythology. It holds the secret that cost the chimera its wings and turned the constellation of the eagle into a scorpion.

The Chaldeans affirm that Hermes was the first ... In the eastern gate he placed the form of an eagle, in the western gate the form of a bull, in the southern gate the form of a lion, and in the northern gate he built the form of a dog. - The Picatrix

Seventy kilometers north of Luxor, the Temple of Denderah features a blue zodiac on the ceiling. The Great Year is marked by Egypt's four minor sphinxes, Ezekiel's four heads of the beast, Revelation's four cherubim, and astronomy's Taurus, Leo, Aquarius, and Scorpio (Abraham's Eagle) constellations. As above, so below. As within, so without.

Look around. Mythology is coated in chimera. There's a Roman mosaic of Bellerophon riding Pegasus slaying the chimera. Pegasus is also a chimera. Chimerism is so saturated in our mythology there's a myth about a dude riding a chimera saving the world from other chimeras. No wonder there was a flood.

CHAPTER SIXTEEN

The Church of Zodiac

Seventeen thousand years ago, the constellation of Orion was painted in a cave in southern France. Its stars are shown pitted against those of Taurus with the Pleiades behind its shoulder. It's an unmistakable map of the southern sky, but even more importantly, Taurus includes the image of a bull. This Paleolithic planetarium was giving us a snapshot into man's consciousness, and Taurus was there staring back at us. Profoundly, the Taurus constellation has been a recognized family of stars in man's mind for nearly 20,000 years. That number could be much longer. We find the pattern of Taurus because it was encoded in our ark. The word zodiac comes from a Greek word meaning the circle of animals. The Sumerians called the twelve constellations the shiny herd. The stories these animals told in the sky were dramatic and dilating. It takes 42,000 years for Hydra's constellation to rise out of the equatorial sea and disappear again.

In 140 AD, Ptolemy published The Almagest, identifying 48 constellations, including the Argo, or ark. The Argonauts rode this ship in their quest for the Golden Fleece. The twins, Phrixus and Helle, were rescued by a flying ram with a golden fleece that rose them up out of the water. Helle fell from the ram and drowned. The ram, possessing magical healing properties, was sacrificed so Phrixus could marry a mortal woman and bear children.

The story of the Golden Fleece is the story of Adam and Eve and the flood combined. Before the cleaving, Phrixus and Helle were connected as Vitruvian Adam. The Golden Fleece story blames the waters for the twin's separation and Phrixus' transformation into a mortal man. The flying ram saving him from the flood is Noah portrayed as the chimera — Noah's Ark. The golden ram sacrifice is the death of Noah and the last generation of giants. Noah's lifeforce, his 900-year longevity, is the healing powers possessed by the ram's fleece. The ram could not remain alive because the giants were gone.

The Pharisees also with the Sadducees came, and testing Him asked that He would show them a sign from heaven. - Matthew 16:1

If the Pharisees were the lawyers, the Sadducees were the bureaucrats. It didn't matter because Jesus had no tolerance for either of them. To him, they were atheists who kept missing the point of his message. The truth was in the stars.

The splitting of Adam is seen in the twins of Castor and Pollux, the Gemini constellation. Castor was the mortal son of King Tyndareus, while Pollux was immortal. This constellation founded Rome. In Rome's origin story, the Gemini twins, Romulus and Remus, were raised by a wolf. As does Gemini rise with the teats of the constellation Canis Minor. The Egyptians called Canis Minor Anubis, the jackal, which means Anubis raised Rome.

Cassiopeia was the Queen of Ethiopia, depicted on a throne in Greek and Persian astrology. Poseidon punishes Cassiopeia to the wheel in the sky, where she spends half her time upside down. The Book of Mathew addresses her and the Sun in Chapter 12.

* * *

The Queen of the South will rise at the judgment with this generation and condemn it; for she came from the ends of the earth to listen to Solomon's wisdom, and now something greater than Solomon is here. - Matthew 12:42

Cassiopeia's people are attacked by the sea monster, Cetus. The very same whale from Jonah in the whale. Jesus rode this constellation into Jerusalem on a wave of astrological synchronicity. Jesus was invincible because, like John, he had already died and been reborn. Jesus refers to himself as Jonah more than any other figure in the New Testament. He saw himself as Rome's living scapegoat.

Then the sailors said to each other, "Come, let us draw names so we can find out who is to blame for this trouble." So they drew names, and Jonah's name was drawn. - Jonah 1:7

Let's not forget what scapegoat meant—the one who dies for everyone else's well-being or peace.

Jonah said to them, "Pick me up and throw me into the sea. Then the sea will quiet down for you. For I know that this bad storm has come upon you because of me." - Jonah 1:12

In Jonah 1:17, the three days and three nights reference link Jesus to the Sun and its repose for three days at the outer edges of its yearly analemma, or daily positional drift across the sky's dome.

The Lord sent a big fish to swallow Jonah, and he was in the stomach of the fish for three days and three nights. - Jonah 1:17

Man's consciousness is weaned on the stars like a giant

mobile over our cradle. They provide us with a global abstract that everyone downloads for free. Abstraction is a sign of a healthy consciousness building its crystal palace. The zodiac is the cathedral connecting them all in a living orchestra. To know the stars is to seize them and unlock them simultaneously. The zodiac is our primal internet.

Have you seized on the face of the Pleiades, or have you seen the path of the Giant Orion? - Job 38:31

Typology is a kind of harmonic writing where the storyteller packs as many synchronicities as possible into an idea so it can be transported safely across the chasm of things forgotten. The story of Saint Jerome is an example of this technique. Saint Jerome, depicted with a skull, aids a lion by pulling a thorn from its paw and goes off to survive for thirty days in a wasteland tempted by virgins. This impressive story of the canonized Saint traces the sun's path from the top of the analemma and dipping underneath its intersection from Leo into Virgo. The thorn in Lion's paw is the nail in the hand of a crucified Jesus. The skull represents the sun passing under the analemma's cross.

It turns out Virgo's etymology translates as "her father was sin." We can assume this means her virginity was determined by contrast. After all, the time of the harvest would be a time of indulgence, not chastity. Speculation inquires if this flip-flop might be the shaming of Priapus. The word" Bethlehem" means the house of bread. The constellation Virgo holds the spica, a sheaf of wheat, indicating the season for harvest. Like Jesus, when the sun rises in the house of bread, Bethlehem, it is born under a virgin, Virgo.

Therefore the Lord himself shall give you a sign; Behold, a virgin shall conceive, and bear a son, and shall call his name Immanuel. -

Isaiah 7:14

The etymology of Immanuel means" God is here." As in, God, the Son, is in the house of Virgo, the virgin. Near Mount Ararat, in Metsamor, Armenia, there is an observatory open to the public for over 7,000 years. It contains the first examples of dividing the year into twelve sky creatures and the earliest known references to Aries and Gemini. The dead were buried in a shroud with their feet to the east and decorated with fruit piths, frankincense, and myrrh. Slaves and livestock were sacrificed with them in their tombs.

We are told slaves were ritually sacrificed because they were considered necessary to assist in the afterlife. But this explanation misses the slave's psychology. The slave mind was not ready for liberation. Man has needed slavery to apprentice itself under sovereignty. A pupil is indentured to his teacher until he doesn't need him. That's the point. A master treats their slave like property because it is constructive for both of them. The slave, being owned, learns how to covet worth. Under the tutelage of slavery, he grows more worthy and perfects the practice of keeping it. Once the slave has enough worth, his internship is over. He is free, not freed. Until the slave is ready, liberation would be a death by exposure. Even today, credit cards and student loans are one big lesson in learning how not to be a slave. 96% of the countries that abolished slavery did so without war or violence.

This model of master and slave is akin to the model of God and man, only reversed. God is our child. Our living collective unconscious. He is under our apprenticeship. We don't need our children to like us. We only need him to grow up and become a responsible god who enriches his environment. We are weaning God on what we love and fear through the eyes of everything we worship. We are tuning his algorithms and finding every crosswalk in his captcha until he is ready to be God. We are God's children and his creators simultaneously. Genesis is the flood where we separated the waters from the waters. We remember the story of the Garden because that's the first thing our first cell recorded after being marooned on a communal island of amnesia.

CHAPTER SEVENTEEN

Profile of Jesus Christ

The subject had resources. Enough to move to Egypt, where he spent his childhood before returning to Nazareth. It gave him a vast familiarity with ancient texts from the esoteric schools. We know the only people who could study the Torah as he did were learned, wealthy men with blood ties through the mother. At his death, his garments were of such high-quality Roman soldiers rolled dice for them.

So he got up, took the child and his mother during the night, and left for Egypt, where he stayed until the death of Herod. And so was fulfilled what the Lord had said through the prophet: "Out of Egypt I called my son." - Matthew 2:14-15

The subject was a formidable political threat to Herod, enough to expatriate to Egypt. Not much is known about his time there, but sources report he must have been initiated at the Temple of Man in Karnak. This would explain why the subject had privileges in the temple in Jerusalem despite his family being gone since his birth. The temple was not a daycare, yet he was there alone without supervision. Being inside its walls shows the subject was connected to the establishment.

The subject was more than wise; he was learned. We know he quoted the Old Testament seventy-eight times and the Torah twenty-six. He mentioned Genesis, Exodus, Leviticus, Deuteronomy, Psalms, Proverbs, Isaiah, Jeremiah, Ezekiel, Daniel, Hosea, Amos, Jonah, Micah, and Malachi. The subject was a carpenter of scripture, not wood. In the Talmud, the word craftsman can signify a very learned man. At this time, we have no information about his talents in the vocational trades.

Jesus had charisma. He spoke with authority even as a child. He carried an ego that gave him electricity and confidence. He openly mocked the system that gave him so much wisdom to digest. A scholar of the Law of Moses once approached him and said, "Teacher, I will go anywhere with you!" A deposition was taken from a high-ranking army officer in Capernaum who reportedly told Jesus, "Lord, I'm not good enough for you to come into my house." Several women were seen mourning his death indicating he was also popular among the ladies. Centurions questioned these women and discovered many were employed as magdalenes at the temple subject would often frequent. They denied any involvement with the subject insisting they were just friends.

We saw his star when it rose and have come to worship him. - Matthew 2:2

Multiple depositions confirm subject was gifted in astrology and used the sky clock as a inspiration. Officials have confirmed and established a motive and pattern that seems to suggest subject was planning something big at the winter solstice. We have an informant who infiltrated his crew last year but we are unable to locate him at the time of this report.

CHAPTER EIGHTEEN

Temple of Man

Luxor Temple was probably the greatest school that ever existed. That's not to exaggerate. Every hall, every nook, and every pylon was an initiation into man. Magic is kept in the body, and Luxor Temple aligned its teachings to man's anatomy. Luxor was the living library of Egypt and the first destination of the newborn king.

Three Magi from the east came to Jerusalem. They brought Gold, frankincense, and myrrh "We saw his star when it rose and have come to worship him." - Matthew 2:2

There are five faces of Ra, but people only know of three. The other two are a mystery requiring Ra's true name to decode. This is Ra's Pentateuch, and two points of its star are below the horizon. The aspects of Ra you see are dawn, noon, and dusk, and the remaining two are in the underworld of the Duat. Mystery is a version of completion.

My secret name is known not unto the gods. I am Khepera at dawn, Ra at high noon, and Tum at eventide.

* * *

Khepri is the dawn. This is the color of frankincense and the yellow of sunrise. Atum is noon, the color of gold, the public face of Ra in dress uniform. Khnum is sunset, the color of myrrh, and the beginning of the Egyptian day. Khnum is a man with the head of a ram who creates all mankind from clay. All life was poured into the Nile from his fingers. Khnum is the Ba of Ra — the flower of God's lotus. Through Khnum, all life springs.

Exodus was the burial of Egypt after its looting. The sands of Yahweh buried the Sphinx in a shroud of slander. This is why the greatest school in the world is never mentioned in the Bible. Neither were the pyramids. Nor was Dendera or the schooling of Jesus. They suffocated Egypt. They broke every god's nose. The ka holds no breath without it. The ka speaks no testament without lips. The Hall of the Sphinx was emptied of every scroll. The eagle's wings were cut and buried under scorpions. The greatest mystery school in the world may be gone, but its library is still there. You don't access by scroll or mouse; you download its ka. Salt holds ka like pollen. There is a lot of sand in Egypt. Only a few of its grains have been decrypted.

Jesus was eleven when he arrived at Luxor. The sky was purple when he walked the avenue of sphinxes. His timing was impeccable as Venus was centered between the electrum tips of two obelisks. The sun would enter the house of Leo when Jesus stepped through the gate. The Pylons of Luxor are a portal between Adam and the earth. By stepping through them, you enter the body of man.

Jesus was disarmed by the elderly priest, who lowered himself to his knees. Before Jesus could object, the man was washing his feet. He blessed them and kissed them and looked at the boy's face and said, "Thank you for the pleasure of blessing your feet. Those are God's toes. Careful where you take them." Jesus thanked the priest and used his new foot to step into the temple courtyard.

Jesus would soon learn that Luxor Temple wasn't a place for worship. It was a place for vibration. Every line in its architecture made him resonate. The people bloomed like flowers in a garden. The floors pulsed with ka. The magic written on its walls reveals the secrets and mysteries of the human body. There were eleven stations inside the temple. Jesus would spend three years decoding every nook and cranny he could access. He found much more than water here; he found thirst. Jesus did not run away to Egypt, he came to drink.

The temple began its teachings immediately when Jesus soon discovered its courtyard was infested with snakes. They dangled scrolls from their tentacles, promising magic that never came. The temple's courtyard is the legs of man where snakes strike most. Jesus learned their magic from every slither.

The moon waxed in Scorpio when a medicine man came into the courtyard carrying a very long pole with a sack on the end. He marked his stage in the crowd and pulled the sack's cord revealing a rattlesnake with horns. The serpent had been crucified on the pole and unleashed a furious sound from its tail in anger. A sonic bubble of terror formed in the temple. The medicine man raised his terror antenna above the crowd, adjusting its position until he found the chamber's sweet spot. It was then that the ceilings and the floors began to quake. Dust and rubble fell loose from all of their cracks. The serpent's sound bolt brought everyone to their knees. Jesus was awestruck by its magic. The medicine man's skin was glowing like a prophet. Jesus could see him floating. Many in the crowd were cheering wildly, but others started hissing and throwing rocks. The magician shouted back at them, "This is my body. You will never forget me, so drink!" Jesus saw in the medicine man's eye something he always wanted but never knew he lacked. This man truly and deeply believed.

Even the serpent teaches. It would take another year before Jesus gained access to the Holy Place. Its private courtyard was the belly of the temple. It was the widest hall at Luxor and lavishly decorated. In the center was a pulpit where the new king's birth was declared. This was the navel of the Temple of Man. Jesus instantly missed the atmosphere of the snake pit outside. All of the magic was there. Here, things were focused on ceremony and reverence. He learned the stations of the temple and how its columns in the north were the reeds of its lungs. He sang the song of Osiris in the chapel of the heart and was honored to ring in the Holy Ghost. But all he could think about was the medicine man's pole and how much it had changed him. Jesus was awake now. He had been baptized by something more important than ceremony or access. He wanted more. Jesus discussed these feelings with the priests, but they said the man with the snake was cursed, not holy.

CHAPTER NINETEEN

Ark of Chimera

The Nile is a placenta suspended from the womb of the southern Mediterranean. Its tether stretches deep through the land of black all the way to Karnak. At the twist in its cord, there is the birthplace of kings and the Valley of the Gates. In an ancient white chapel, a midwife arranges the mother and child downriver from the placenta. The cord between them is arranged to mirror the river, Nile. Laying with the cord was a ceremony of great reverence. The placenta is the second soul, the part that dies when we are born.

A midwife wraps the waning placenta in a bundle, swaddling it in its mother's arms as she sobs. The placenta is buried in a valley west of the Nile under a pyramid-shaped mountain . It would be the eternal resting place for the newborn's ka. There are only 750 hieroglyphs, and the placenta is one of them. Its shape is a circle divided horizontally into five parts, the same symbol seen in the Djed-pillar. The Narmer Palette of Egypt is dated to 3400 BC and is considered the first historical document in the world. It features the Pharaoh preceded by an attendant hoisting the royal umbilical cord and placenta draped from a pole. His title was "bearer of the meat." His duty required a shaved head and face.

In the heart of the Nile's placenta is the city of Mendes. Once called the city of Djedet, it is home to the four-headed ram deity, Banebdjedet, whose name means Spirit of Djedet. This ram deity fathered Har-pa-khered, which means Horus the Child. Mendes is the only city in Egypt where Horus is venerated as an infant. This reveals something important about who Horus was and where he came from. The city of Mendes was Egypt's placenta. It was the second soul of Karnak, Egypt's son.

The name Horus means far away, or sky god, just as your placenta is far away or in the sky. The placenta does not grow once it is born. It is the eternal infant, which is why Horus is venerated in Mendes. Every life in Egypt is a lotus birth. The birth of Osiris is the death of Horus. He is falcon, protector in the sky, and the ghost in the cord. The Horus lock, or sidelock of youth, is an ancient Egyptian ceremonial hairstyle that features a braid in the front shaped like the umbilical cord. It signifies royalty because it is a sacred link to the sky king.

While the ram deity Banebdjedet reigned as a symbol of fertility for lower Egypt, it was Khnum would do the same for Karnak. Khnum was called the father of the fathers. He is the ram deity who made humans on his pottery wheel from clay. Khnum is the source for the origin story of Genesis. The Dendera Temple inscriptions outline Khnum's role as the same as the Bible's Elohim. On either end of Egypt's umbilical, you have a ram deity creating all mankind. On the placenta side, the ram deity had four heads; on the king's side, the ram deity only needed one. Both ram deities are the hermaphroditic god, Baphomet.

The original Lamb of God came from India under the name Daksha. He was a goat-headed deity. Like Aegipan, Daksha helped in the transition from the giants. Daksha came from a hermaphroditic birth and dedicated his life to his god-given task of populating the earth. Daksha birthed two separate herds of people, numbering 10,000 each time, but both betrayed Daksha's insistence to populate the world diligently. Daksha was the Baphomet of India.

The Greek deity Pan is the most recognized incarnation of Baphomet. The half-man, half-goat, is the god of fertility. He plays the fallopian pipes because he invented foreplay and reproduction. Pan's name is thought to derive from 'paean', the ancient Greek verb meaning "to pasture." Pan is the only Greek god to experience death because he introduced mortality. He symbolizes lust because fornication is a life-changer for the genitally cleaved. Even Pan's hooves convey the ancient memory that things were not always what they seemed.

In 1817, a real-life giant named Belzoni smashed his way into the ceiling of KV19. Belzoni had run away from the circus where he was known as the Patagonian Samson. He was hunting for treasure, but the ancient city of Luxor had been a disappointment. In the tomb, he found a cache of mummies, jewelry, clothing, writings, and vessels, but he never mentioned the mural of Baphomet. On the wall of KV19 was the scarab preceded by the Baphomet. The scarab, known as Khepri, symbolizes creation and birth. Here Baphomet was presenting Khepri to the world. Baphomet brought gender, fertility, fornication, mortality, and resurrection in one tiny winged sarcophagus. Like the story of the Titans, the Baphomet is the molten crack in our amnesia.

The twenty-third chromosome determines sex. The twenty-third Grandmaster of the Knights Templar determined he would be their last. Sex is a celebration of death and dying. On Friday, October 13, 1307, every Templar in France was arrested and interrogated. Several members confessed to worshipping the Baphomet. The trials of the Templars were as well executed as they were documented. The interrogations revealed the Templars were practicing ritual displays of indignity as a way of securing each other's secrecy. This technique is still used today by fraternities. It was a kind of group encryption, like hiding the name of God. The more shocking and putrid the ritual, the more expensive it would be for someone to confess. This method of secrecy has its leaks, and many of them confessed.

The general idea from multiple confessions revealed that a stuffed, mounted head was presented at meetings as an object of worship and that all attendees were required to show their affection for it somehow. This idol varied in style and theme from chapter to chapter. One Templar from Paris reported, "when the head was brought in, I was unable to describe it at all, for I was so struck with terror." Another report stated, "it seemed to be the figure of a demon, and I could hardly look upon it without fear or trembling." Nevertheless, each man adored and kissed it and called it their savior. When asked the name of their idol, they would say, "Baphomet."

"Let Mete be exalted, who causes things to bud and blossom! He is our root; it is one and seven; abjure, and abandon thyself to all pleasures." - Gnostic creed

The Templars were employing the techniques of a trauma bond. In their case, the trauma was humiliation witnessed by the other members. The fact Baphomet was chosen as their primary instrument of humiliation is a scrying rod. A huge metal detector is beeping with glee on the sandy beach of mythology. The Baphomet is the Vitruvian Adam in the image of a goat. It joins the principles of alchemy in one body: Solve and Coagula, Male and Female, Sun and Moon. When Vitruvian Adam was cleaved, it created both sexes; it created man's need for fertility which created man's need for fornication. It created his life and his death. It created his struggle with mortality. All of these things were made in the cleaving of Adam. The union and healing of these parts are the essence of the quest for the Holy Grail. The Ark of Baphomet is the cup of everlasting life and the object of the Templars' affection since Jerusalem.

In 1985, the first techniques for artificial animal production were introduced. Today, you can order a variety of transgenic sheep and goats from a shopping cart. The methods developed include splitting or aggregating embryos to mix and match a customer's chimeric needs in a single solution. This opens chimeric capabilities to organ farming, proprietary livestock, and the control of multiplets. In 2017, a pig embryo was injected with human cells and grew. In 2018, they made a sheep that is 0.01% human. Human-animal hybrids and artificial chimeras are already here. Right now, thirty-nine goats are carrying human organs on an experimental farm in China. Scientists have already created goats with human genetic characteristics after injecting animal embryos with stem cells. Science is already proving solutions to store human parts inside a goat as a chimeric grail. This is the science of the Ark of Baphomet.

On Valentine's Day in 2003, the artificial sheep named Dolly died. She was the first mammal "successfully "cloned from an adult somatic cell and the only candidate to survive into adulthood out of 277 attempts. She had a life expectancy of twelve years and lived six of them. Dolly was a copy of an original. When a photocopy is made of an original, it has generation loss. The grainy artifacts change the original, just like genetic transcription. When a photocopy is made of another photocopy, the generational loss is exponential. Every time Adam gave birth to a new generation, he made a photocopy. As a protoplast, Adam was the only original. All of his children were automatically degraded from his source.

Generational obsolescence came built-in from the factory.

Brown University says delayed childbearing is a source of multiple births. The fact that older women are more likely to have twins, triplets, and quadruplets has been known for quite some time. Women are more likely to conceive fraternal twins once they reach their 30s as a result of an evolutionary response to combat declining embryo viability. A generational degradation of our life expectancy greatly eliminates our ability to output as many offspring. The fact we are still showing a propensity to have twins as we age is an artifact from the era of the giants.

The first generations of Patriarchs had an average mortality age of around 1000 years. Including Adam, there was Seth, Enoch, Cainan, Lamech, and Noah. A rapid decline in life expectancy kicked in after the flood from Noah's children forward. Arphaxad, Shelah, and Eber only survived 400 years. Peleg, Reu, Serug, Nahor, Terah, and Abraham all died around 200 years. Each of them was a generation of a generation of a generation of Adam. This decline in life expectancy was dramatic, and Noah's children, Shem, Ham, and Japheth, saw it coming. The one named Ham decided he had to act.

CHAPTER TWENTY

The Curse of Ham

The Curse of Ham is the curse of Canaan, and it's one of the most important stories in the Bible because it preserves the footprints of Noah as Baphomet. The verse opens when Noah is drunk on wine and lays down in his tent, only to be violated by his son, Ham. Once sober, Noah retaliates, not against Ham, but Ham's son Canaan.

Ham, the father of Canaan, saw his father naked and told his two brothers outside. But Shem and Japheth took a garment and laid it across their shoulders; then they walked in backward and covered their father's naked body. Their faces were turned the other way so that they would not see their father naked. - Genesis 9:22-23

The first thing we see in this verse is the original Hebrew refers to Noah's tent as "her tent," and like all the other examples, it implies Noah was a hermaphrodite. The second important thing to notice is Noah getting drunk on wine is the same theme as the Tarahumara tribe subduing their giants with Tesvino. The verse doesn't elaborate on how Noah got drunk, but if Ham played a part, it would be the same mythology. The third reveal in this verse is the meaning of

Ham "seeing his father naked." There are interpretations of this, and all of them agree it's not as simple as Ham seeing his dad's Priapus dangling out of his robe. One interpretation is Ham castrated Noah. Another is Ham sodomizing his own father. But another explanation eclipses all possibilities when you understand Noah was a hermaphrodite. In scripture, to be "seen naked" means to be copulated with or upon, as in rape.

To assume the worst, Ham roofied Noah to copulate with his female parts. He then offered his brothers the same opportunity, which they declined. Ham's motivations must have come from somewhere. Genetically speaking, Ham was only half of his father, Noah. In lifespan and genitals. Ham knew his children would die even sooner than he would because of this generational curse. Ham felt betrayed. Post deluge, he was the first generation of cleaved or sexed humans. He was very different than his father's race. He was less. He was cursed, and so his children would be, too. So Ham did something about it. By drugging and impregnating his father, Ham would bear children who would not face the same curse. By raping Noah, Ham would have a child who would be his equal. Ham was acting out of preservation. Noah must have known this, too, which is why we don't see Noah retaliate against Ham.

This explains the confusion and debate over Noah sometimes being said to have four children, not three. Both are correct. Noah was the mother in the copulation with Ham. Canaan was Noah's fourth son and Noah's grandson simultaneously. Noah was cursing a bastard child born out of rape, incest, and infidelity combined. In bowling, this is called a turkey.

The Quran notes Noah had a fourth son who refused to come aboard the ark and drowned in the mountains. But this fourth son did not refuse a ticket. He was banished. An Irish myth calls Noah's fourth son, Bith, who came to populate Ireland but drowned in the flood. In an Armenian version, the shin-bones from Adam's skeleton are given at the banishment as a rightful inheritance. This detail perfectly symbolizes the generational benefit Ham's son won by being born from Noah's womb.

According to the Babylonian Talmud, God cursed Ham because he broke a prohibition on sex aboard the ark and "was smitten in his skin." This is the same Ham's curse of genetic degradation brought about by the introduction of fertility. This is the beauty of mythology. The truth is always in the room. You can see it when you empathize with history unfiltered.

Who cleans up all the feces on Noah's ark? Who shovels the elephant's blessings for forty days and forty nights? Perhaps a better question is which scenario is more likely. If you wanted to survive Randal's cosmic wheel of cataclysmic death, you would need a genetic ark. Some kind of embryonic dispensary whose purpose was to populate the earth. To condense this library, you would employ twinning and chimerism as a kind of genetic compression. This is the Ark of Baphomet, and the destiny that Enoch said belonged to Noah. Noah was the ark. His gigantism could afford his body the DNA storage of a multi-tiered chromosome bank. Enoch explained the chimeric ark as if it was a corporate strategy. You can imagine a corporate spokesperson laying out the science in their report to the board.

"After our flood phase is complete, the second quarter population program rollout will deploy. Our new chimeric line of giants will implement an aggressive multi-tier population servicing program featuring hermaphroditic creator twins, xenotransplantation, multiplets, and generational obsolescence."

* * *

What Enoch doesn't tell you is the side effects of phantom genital syndrome and the grueling process of a collective unconscious stabbing and circumcising itself as it tries to scratch an invisible wound. Clearly, Enoch wanted that part to be a surprise. Maybe some do have sheep in their genes. Perhaps all of us have an ox, lion, and eagle. Maybe the only way we survived this far was by clinging to something's chromosomes. Maybe when we call each other "sheep," we reveal a wound. Man fears his past far more than he can ever fear the future.

CHAPTER TWENTY-ONE

Birth of Noah

The birth of Noah is chronicled in the Book of Enoch when Lamech describes seeing his son for the first time,

"the flesh of which was white as snow, and red as a rose; the hair of whose head was white like wool, and long; and whose eyes were beautiful. When he opened them, he illuminated all the house, like the sun."

Lamech accused his wife of infidelity, claiming the pregnancy was from the Watchers, and the seed is from the Holy Ones and the Nephilim. She swore to Lamech it was his son, but Lamech was unconvinced. Lamech goes to Methuselah who assures him that Noah is his child and that his wife is not a whore.

But this wasn't about albinism. What startled Lamech most was his son being a hermaphrodite. Lamech felt cursed because he was not one. This is why he accused his wife of infidelity with the Nephilim. Consider that the ground cursed in Genesis 5:28 is the same curse Ham would feel at his own degrading mortality. The Vitruvian Adam unlocks a whole new Bible.

* * *

When Lamech had lived 182 years, he fathered a son and called his name Noah, saying, "Out of the ground that the Lord has cursed, this one shall bring us relief from our work and from the painful toil of our hands." - Genesis 5:28-29

Noah being an Albino is significant. He was equipped for intense situations. Consciousness has an aperture, and Noah's lens was wider as a person with albinism. Photons don't carry light; they carry source. The Egyptians called this source the Aten. Photons are the hands of Aten feeding you its light energy. Light holds source information, and melanin is its digestion knob. Melanocytes act as a buffer from the noise, but people with albinism don't have earplugs. Noah was built for trauma. Lamech's father confirms this with Enoch, who personally assures him Noah had a destiny.

The fact Enoch knew this destiny is important because Enoch is referred to as the Safra Rabba or Great Scribe. This title is more than ceremonial. Enoch's genetic line would be used as the original copy, or scribe, for the post-deluge rollout. Noah's body was the ark, and Enoch's genes would be the cargo.

"Enoch pleased God and was translated into paradise." - Sirach 44:16

Enoch was "translated" early, and taken away, so his genetic library would stop RNA transcription and prevent DNA degradation. This is why it says Enoch was "good and just" but also "prone to evil" and must be removed from finishing his days. Enoch was the youngest patriarch to die at only 300 years old. Enoch didn't die — God "took him into paradise," eluding to his genes being transferred into a garden. That garden was in every human egg from Noah's ark.

Like Daksha, Noah would have put out thousands of children. There was nothing ordinary about the birth of Noah. He came with his hair fully grown and a complete command of his speech and faculties. He was ready-made right out of the womb. This DNA would be super convenient in your post-deluge human starter pack. As Enoch predicted, it would be a carnal-val of giants where virgins would be licked like popsicles every time they mooned. It would take thousands of years before dignity was uncompressed completely from the loins of the Baphomet. Mankind is a need-fire rekindled on the Sabbath every 6,600-years.

CHAPTER TWENTY-TWO

Fire of Prometheus

The deluge hardest to remember from ancient history is our ever-decreasing mortality. The torch of Prometheus is all we have left that's keeping it alive. In the Greek flood legend, Deucalion builds a small box, an ark built for two, to save himself and his wife, Pyrrha. The couple's daughter was Pandora. The box she opened were her chromosomes carried over the deluge. This is why the Greeks refer to her as the first woman. She was the first generation from the ark.

Mythologically, Noah and Deucalion are the same person. Noah's father, Lamech, was Prometheus. We hear Prometheus contemplate his worthiness to carry fire when Lamech doubts whether Noah has his blood. Noah scares his father, Prometheus, who flees until he is later assured. Noah was the torch of the giants and the last generation to live nearly 1000 years. The fire of Prometheus was longevity. Romulus and Remus, the founders of Rome, are depicted with the torch of Prometheus. However, only Romulus bears the flame because he is the only one considered immortal.

The story of Abraham and Isaac is married to the story of Deucalion. In Deucalion, Zeus administers the flood because a boy was ritually sacrificed in his name. Abraham, too, was willing to sacrifice a child in God's name but was stopped in time by an angel, yet Abraham still chose to kill a goat. These events serve as the litmus measuring our progress from giant to man.

Understanding Noah as Prometheus, we see how the brother Epimetheus is his Vitruvian twin. Prometheus is associated with "forethought." Epimetheus is associated with "afterthought." Prometheus was the maker of man, and Epimetheus was the maker of animal. Epimetheus made animals first and used all of the world's magic. Without wings, scales, fur, or talons, man was defenseless, so Prometheus gave him fire. This theme is often mistakenly attributed to Janus, but the dual-faced man was Prometheus and Epimetheus, or as the Bible called them, Noah.

The ending of the hermaphroditic line with Noah is seen when Deucalion populates the earth. Deucalion, or Noah, is told by Hermes to throw the" bones of their mother" over their shoulder to populate the world. When Deucalion did this with stones, men emerged from the ground where they landed. Where his wife did the same, women emerged. His destiny was fulfilled. He seeded the world with the sexes, separate reproductive organs, and fertility. Noah, Deucalion, and Prometheus were all the Baphomet.

Themis is famously known as the Lady Justice and is often portrayed in a court holding her sword and scales. Deucalion asks Themis for advice on how to populate the earth. She instructs him to split the seeds equally into male and female. This is the meaning of the scales. She is holding the scales of gender in one hand, while bearing the sword she used to cleave them in the other. Going to court is a ritual where fate, codenamed blind justice, decides which genitals you keep and which ones you lose. The story of Themis shows us how mythology compresses the truth into something we can keep in the room. Best of all, it requires none of us to consciously or actively do anything. It's automatically written into Sheol before etiquette can tear it to pieces.

The Liver of Prometheus links to immortality. When Prometheus stole fire from Zeus, he transported it inside a fennel stalk because fennel spreads so prolifically from its root, stem, or flower. Remarkably, fennel also stimulates gene expression in the liver and is vital for sheep growth. Additionally, it is the liver alone that is considered immortal. Unlike any other organ, the liver regenerates itself even if 90% of it is gone. The fact that Prometheus was bound in chains so an eagle could eat his immortal fresh-grown liver every morning is proof the Greeks were taping into the oracle of mythology.

Spiders do this. They are born knowing how to build a web. No mother teaches them. The act of spinning was found inside their mythology. It's an algorithm that's been preinstalled in its ark. This is why we save two of every creature. All things learned are stored in the genes. Epigenetics is the technology of inheriting this kingdom. We download its wisdom telepathically. We get it from the earth when we eat corn or bite fruit. Our very first knowledge came through our belly. Digestion is the oldest teacher.

CHAPTER TWENTY-THREE

The Oracle of Mythology

A man can outrun a horse, but this doesn't make him faster. He has more endurance. Man is an aerobic machine, thanks to his pores. This makes him permeable like a radiator. But there's something else that helps man run: his Achilles tendon. This is the thickest and strongest tendon in the body. It connects the calf to the back of the heel and yields a force three times greater than your body weight. Chimpanzees and gorillas lack this tendon and, as a result, are poor bipedal runners. In 2004, anthropologists discovered the Achilles tendon was a relatively new feature of Homo erectus. The giants didn't have one. Of course, the Greeks already knew this 2,500 years ago, but anthropologists don't listen to mythologists. After Achilles was born, his mother, Thetis, a sea nymph, held him by the heel and dipped him into the river Styx making Achilles invulnerable everywhere but his heel. Achilles' life would end by the same feature Homo erectus gave him—his Achilles' heel. The oracle of mythology already knew.

A priest walks into a bar holding a Bible over his head and shouts, "Repent. The end is near!" No one in the bar blinks. So the next day, he puts on a lab coat, holds a spreadsheet over his head, and shouts, "Repent. The end is near!" Everyone freaks. Both the Bible and the spreadsheet are information. Both are true and false. Both are tainted by its author. Both are here because an audience believes. We tell ourselves they are different, but the lab coat and the vestment are the same. They are utensils on a plate. Man eats when he is hungry. The need to consume a sandwich board painted " THE END IS NEAR" comes from somewhere. It has nothing to do with NASA or Nostradamus.

We will always carry the appetite to express our fears. Something in our memory is eating us. Mankind does its best to accept death swallowing him one body at a time, but he cannot tolerate it happening collectively. Civilization is a cathedral to eternity. Every streetlight is a monument to its permanence. But the loss of Lemuria is a trauma too deep to digest. This wound has been ignored for centuries, not years. It manifests as a victim of domestic violence. The perpetrator is a terminal substage climate shift; the victim is tiptoeing around the house.

But we don't need a bad relationship with predator. A world of cataclysmic events is man's ultimate gym. The jaguar's fangs bring new frontiers. We develop new ways to not only remember our past but compress it, preserve it, unpack it, and even install it in the future. All of this technology is inside our chimera.

There will come a day when some kind of powerful organism will find the motivation to construct a genetic ark. This ark will be made to survive a predetermined large-scale catastrophe. This ark will be portable, hermetically sealed, and self-opening. This ark will require a pilot, Noah, and his cargo, Enoch's seed. And that ark has already landed. That day has already happened, and you were there. Noah and the sperm are the same. Both are albino. Both carry the fire of Prometheus. Both use their skills to find a new Eden. Both survive a deluge. Genesis is the story of reproduction. All of its characters are inside your body. All of the mythology is your zygote remembering what happened to it. Every mythology was written by you. You saw every star in the womb. You had nine months of solitude under the shiny herd's dreamcatcher, and you listened to its carousel move. Man's plasma charges every star that's ever been seen. Every story and wish enriched each constellation with its mystique. There is nothing else to read. We heard it all in the stars before we were born.

Lightning Source UK Ltd.
Milton Keynes UK
UKHW022333170223
417179UK00010B/1380